Buddharakkhita

Jinalankara

Buddharakkhita

Jinalankara

ISBN/EAN: 9783337385095

Printed in Europe, USA, Canada, Australia, Japan

Cover: Foto ©Andreas Hilbeck / pixelio.de

More available books at **www.hansebooks.com**

JINÂLAṄKÂRA

OR

"EMBELLISHMENTS OF BUDDHA"

BY

BUDDHARAKKHITA

EDITED, WITH INTRODUCTION, NOTES, AND TRANSLATION

BY

JAMES GRAY

PROFESSOR OF PALI, RANGOON COLLEGE
AND AUTHOR OF "BUDDHAGHOSUPPATTI," "THE NÎTI
LITERATURE OF BURMA," ETC.

LONDON
LUZAC & CO., GREAT RUSSELL STREET
PUBLISHERS TO THE INDIA OFFICE
1894

TABLE OF CONTENTS

INTRODUCTION

A HIGH antiquity is accorded to the *Jinâlaṅkâra*. The postscript to the text ascribes the authorship to Buddharakkhita, who is stated to have been born in Ceylon of a distinguished family in the 117th year of the *nirvâṇa* of Buddha, *i.e.*, in B.C. 426. His birthplace was Rohana, and it appears that he was the head of a congregation of priests in Coḷikatambaraṭṭha (afterwards Tambamaṇi), the maritime western division of Ceylon, where the Coḷas of the Coromandel coast originally settled. His learning and quick-wittedness acquired for him a considerable reputation, which traditional history has preserved to the present day.

Accepting the date of Buddharakkhita given above as correct, we must ascribe the text to a period nearly a century before the reign of Tissa, better known as Devânampiyatissa, in whose reign Mahinda, after the Council of Pâṭaliputra, came as missionary apostle to Ceylon, bringing with him the authorised version of the Buddhist scriptures, with their commentaries. That island had become a field for missionary work in the first century after the death of Buddha. It had come under Brahmanic influence some time before, and with the establishment of the colony from Bengal under the rule of Vijaya, in B.C. 527 (a date supported by Burmese chronology), good scope must have presented itself for the spread of the Buddhist faith that had been but lately received with favour in the Gangetic delta, although Vijaya himself was less concerned with religious affairs than with the economic development of the territory acquired by him.

Buddharakkhita probably sprang from a family that had settled in south-eastern Ceylon and migrated to Tambamaṇi when the colony from Bengal had secured a proper footing. It was in all likelihood of the Mâgadha race, for Buddharakkhita is represented by his commentator as writing for the Mâgadhese in particular. With the inducements to missionary work in Vijaya's domain, our author must have joined the church, and as an outcome of his devotion to Pali studies, composed the *Jinâlaṅkâra*.

The name of the treatise signifies "Embellishments of the Conqueror," and is sufficiently indicated in the following stanza:—

Ñâṇâsinâ titikkhena jitamârabalaṁ jinaṁ
Jinâlaṅkâra nâmena âlaṅkârena 'laṅkari.

"He (Buddharakkhita), by the adornment known as *Jinâlaṅkâra*, adorned the Conqueror (Buddha), who, with the sharp sword of knowledge, overcame the forces of Mâra." The commentator, moreover, describes the author as a "Treasurer" (Bhaṇḍagârika) who, taking the attributes of Buddha, deposits them in the scented basket *Jinâlaṅkâra*. "Buddharakkhitâcariyo sabbalokissarassa anantajinassa Buddhassa bhagavato guṇâlaṅkârabhaṇḍâni gahetvâ Jinâlaṅkârassa saṅkhâte gandhakaraṇḍake pakkhipetvâ punnâyakaratanasadissa yogâvacarakulaputtassa niyyâdesi."

In the flourishing days of Buddhistic literature in Burma the text was studied in every monastery of importance, but it is now much neglected, and copies are becoming rare. Its reputation as an ancient work composed by an able scholar in unique style is, however, still maintained through an excellent *Ṭîkâ*, which, as a storehouse of much information in connection with the life and teachings of Buddha, is held in high appreciation by native scholars. Of its value as an important work of reference, Burnouf in his "Lotus" has given us ample evidence. Its author, Buddhadatta, was the contemporary of Buddhaghosa the great commentator. There seems to have been an older *Ṭīkā* by Buddharakkhita himself, but that is not extant. It is difficult to assign any precise reason for its disappearance, as it is for the fragmentary manner in which the *Jinālaṅkāra* has come down to us. The text and Buddhadatta's gloss as we now have them were in existence in Burma before the destruction of the Sinhalese manuscripts by the Malabars, so that there must have been some causes at work in Ceylon itself at an earlier period than the twelfth century which led to the loss to which I have referred. Possibly the attention devoted to the study of the commentaries, introduced into the island by Mahinda, may have relegated the *Jinālaṅkāra* into comparative oblivion. It is due to Buddhadatta that the present text, however incomplete, has been preserved. He had, as we are told in more places than one, a partiality for secular or semi-sacred literature in connection with Buddhism; and during his stay in Ceylon, before returning to Magadha, he transcribed a copy and provided it with a commentary (*Ṭīkā*). As a reference to the *Visuddhimagga* occurs in the latter, it must have been written subsequent to Buddhaghosa's visit to Ceylon. This statement, however, it must be acknowledged, scarcely harmonises with the account of Buddhadatta's and Buddhaghosa's meeting as recorded in the *Buddhaghosuppatti*. I am inclined to think that they met in Ceylon, and that Buddhadatta must have then seen his contemporary's great encyclopædic work. Of the three hundred stanzas in the original *Jinālaṅkāra*, only two hundred and fifty have come down intact. The sections of the work, however, seem identical with the divisional arrangement of the treatise as made by Buddharakkhita.

Here I draw attention to the designation "aṭṭhakathâ" as applied to the *Jinâlankâra* of Buddharakkhita. Burmese authorities describe it as such, which would show that the term had a wider signification than is usually allowed. Any treatise of a Buddhistic character, whether a narrative of Buddha's life to illustrate the Piṭaka or an exegetical work to expound its doctrines, seems to have been called an "aṭṭhakathâ." When, therefore, we read of the *aṭṭhakathas* of the great teachers and elders of the early Buddhist church, we must take them to be not only commentaries in our acceptation of the term, but treatises of a more general character in relation to Buddhism. Buddharakkhita, no doubt, finding his *Jinâlankâra* somewhat abstruse in its poetical form, furnished it with a gloss (Ṭîkâ), which, in works of Pali bibliography, is referred to as the "Old Ṭîkâ." If any indirect testimony were wanted to prove the antiquity of the *Jinâlankâra*, no better could be adduced than the circumstance of its being called an "aṭṭhakathâ."

A high rhetorical value is conceded to the *Jinâlankâra* by native scholars. Its diction is marked by elegance and brilliancy. The style throughout is concise and vigorous, while for rhythmical cadence and variety of versification it stands unrivalled. What the *Milinda-pañha* is to prose, that the *Jinâlankâra* is in the domain of Pali poetry. As a Buddhistic treatise it stands unique as departing from the conventional style of the Piṭaka books. What makes it particularly so is the introduction of artificially constructed stanzas in the style of Kâlidâsa, Bhâravi, and Mâgha. It would be conceding too much to affirm that Mâgadhese was the earliest medium in India for the exhibition in its literature of paragram and paranomasia, of rhyme, alliteration, and palindrome, and other such rhetorical devices. The date, however, of Buddharakkhita would indicate that the artificial style of composition was in vogue in the fourth century B.C., and that, if he is to be looked upon as an imitator of

Sanskrit writers, the authors of *Râghuvaṁsa* and *Kirâtârjunîya* must have flourished not after the commencement of the Christian era, but at least four centuries before. Several parallels may be noticed between the artificial stanzas in their works, and those occurring in the *Jinâlaṅkâra*. Stanzas 49–110 in the latter furnish examples of the artificial style. Attention is here drawn to a few. The following illustrates the use of internal rhyme:—

> Disvâ nimittâni madacchidâni
> thînaṁ virûpâni ratacchidâni
> pâpâni kammâni sukhacchidâni
> laddhâni ñâṇâni bhavacchidâni. (*v.* 49.)

The underlined parts of the words will sufficiently indicate the nature of the rhyme. Here is another in almost similar style:—

> Nânâsanâni sayanâni nivesanâni
> bhûbhanibhâni ratanâkarasannibhâni
> tatrussitâni ratanaddhajabhûsitâni
> hitvâ va tâni himabindusamâni tâni. (*v.* 85.)

The following is paragrammatic:—

> Tathâgataccheramahosi tassa
> tathâ himaropitadâhasantiṁ
> tathâ hi Mâro pi tadâha santiṁ
> tathâ hi mâropi tadâ hasantiṁ. (*v.* 96.)

The following furnish examples of what may be termed paragrammatic echoing rhymes:—

> (*a.*) Padittagehâ viya bheravaṁ ravaṁ
> ravaṁ samuṭṭhâya gato mahesi
> mahesimolokayaputtamattano
> tanosi no pemamahoghamattano. (*v.* 50.)

(*b*.) Disvâna dukkhânalasambhavaṁbhavaṁ
katvâ taduppâdakanaṅgabhaṅgaṁ
Yasodharaṁ pîṇapayodharâdharaṁ
hitvâ gato buddhabalappadaṁ padaṁ. (*v.* 93.)

The following stanza is constructed of synonymous quarter-verses:—

Sakâmadâtâ vinayâmanantagû
Sakâmadâtâ vinayâmanantagû
sakâmadâtâ vinayâmanantagû
sakâmadâtâ vinayâmanantagû. (*v.* 97.)

Alliteration of one or more consonants is exemplified in stanzas 105–108. Sanskrit scholars will recognise a parallel in the following:—

Nonânino nanûnâni nanenâni nanânino
nunnânenâni nûna na nânanaṁ nânanena no. (*v.* 105.)

The use of the palindrome is exemplified in the following:—

Râjarâjayasopetavisesaṁ racitaṁ mayâ
yâmataṁ cirasaṁsevitapeso yajarâjara. (*v.* 100.)

The following curious invocation, which introduces the artificially constructed stanzas, also reads the same forward and backward:—

"Namo tassa yato mahimato yassa tamo na."

"Honour to him (Buddha) inasmuch as to him deserving of honour no darkness is!"

The following, as an illustration of the synonymous and echoing rhyme, is peculiar:—

Raveraverorabhimârabherave
raveraverariva bherave rave
rave rave sûditagârave rave
raveravedesi jinorave rave. (*v.* 98.)

The object of the stanza is to display the same sound at the beginning and the end of each quarter-verse.

In the following all the gutturals are brought into play throughout the stanza:—

> Âkaṅkhakkhâkaṅkhaṅga kaṅkhâgaṅgâkhâgâhaka
> Kaṅkhâgâhakakaṅkhâgha hâ hâ kaṅkhâ kahaṁ kahaṁ.
> (*v.* 101.)

Here the vowels *a* and *â* are treated as gutturals as in the phonetic system of Pâṇini, as well as *h* and *ṁ*. This stanza is important as indicating the true phonetic values of those letters in the ancient speech of Mâgadha.

It appears strange that the artificial style of composition should have been foisted upon a work of a religious character. Books on rhetoric rightly condemn the levity of the practice, especially in relation to serious subjects. Buddharakkhita's performance in that direction was, no doubt, a concession to the taste of the times in which he lived, although now liable to the same disapprobation as the word-jingles of the *Paradise Lost*. We, at this distance of time, will look upon the artificial stanzas of the *Jinâlaṅkâra* in the light of literary curiosities, and be content to recognise in the Mâgadha language a potentiality for the expression of thought possessed by Sanskrit, and which might have, under circumstances different from those that determined the literary development of the language, been the means of producing as extensive a literature as Sanksrit itself.

The *Jinâlaṅkâra* displays much versatility in its versification. In addition to the common *Vatta* class of metres with its subdivision the *Pathyâvatta*, there are eleven varieties, viz.—*Saddharâ*, *Indavajirâ*, *Upavajirâ*, *Vaṁsaṭṭha*, *Vasantatilakâ*, *Dodhakaṁ*, *Toṭaka*, *Mandakkantâ*, *Vijjummâla*, *Malinî*, and *Saddâlavikkîḷitî*. A large proportion of the stanzas are *Upajâti*, chiefly composed of *Indavajira* and *Upavajira* verses, while the *Indavaṁsa* measure comes in occasionally in the quarter-verses and, in one instance, the *Kamalâ*. I have given a scheme of the metres employed, because it is when attention is paid to the versification the beauties of harmony and rhythm make themselves apparent, and the reading of the text becomes a veritable pleasure. The following stanza, for instance, has the musical ring of "The Destruction of Sennacherib" if read with due attention to the metre:—

Sanarâmarubrahmaganebhi rutâ
arahâdigunâ vipulâ vimalâ
navadhâ vasudhâgagaṇe gahaṇâ
Sakale tidive tibhave visaṭâ. (*v.* 180.)

The metre is *Toṭaka* ⏑ ⏑ — | ⏑ ⏑ — | ⏑ ⏑ — | ⏑ ⏑ — |, the same as that of Byron's beautiful poem. The following are also in the same metre, though more monotonous in movement than the one just quoted:—

Bhajitaṁ cajitaṁ pavanaṁ bhavanaṁ
jahitaṁ gahitaṁ samalaṁ amalaṁ
sugataṁ agataṁ sugatiṁ agatiṁ
namitaṁ amitaṁ namatiṁ sumatiṁ. (*v.* 173.)

Munirâjavaro nararâjavaro
dividevavaro sucibrahmavaro
sakapâpaharo parapâpaharo
sakavuḍḍhikaro paravuḍḍhikaro. (*v.* 179.)

Then take the *Dodhakam* — ⏑ ⏑ | — ⏑ ⏑ | — ⏑ ⏑ | — ⏑ ⏑ |. The following half-stanza would be tame unless read with a knowledge of its metrical structure:—

Rammasurammasubhesu gharesu
tiṇṇamutûnamanucchavikesu. (*v.* 48.)

The *Mattâsamaka* class of metres, such as the *Vetâlîya Gîti*, &c., is, strange to say, not represented in Buddharakkhita's poem. Irregularities of versification are comparatively rare, and have been pointed out by me.

The study of the text requires some familiarity with the life and teachings of Buddha. The *Ṭīkā* I have used is a useful work of reference in this respect, but the work being voluminous, it was beside my immediate purpose to furnish an appendix of extracts from it. I may, however, have occasion hereafter to bring it to use for the benefit of Pali students. For the redaction of the text of *Jinālaṅkāra* I have had five manuscripts at my service, two copies of the *Ṭīkā* and the *Gulatthadīpanī*. I have not thought it necessary to specialise the different copies of the text now edited by me, as they do not present any marked divergences. Different readings have been indicated in the course of the notes.

JINÂLAṄKÂRA

CONTENTS OF THE TEXT

JINÂLAṄKÂRA

Namo tassa bhagavato arahato sammâsambuddhassa.

I. Paṇâmadîpanîgâthâ.

1 Yo lokatthâya Buddho dhanasutabhariyâaṅgajîve cajitvâ
pûretvâ pâramîyo tidasamanupame bodhipakkhiya-
dhamme
patvâ bodhiṁ visuddhaṁ sakalaguṇadadaṁ seṭṭhabhûto
tiloke
katvâ dukkhassa antaṁ katasubhajanataṁ dukkhato
mocayittha.

2 Natvânâhaṁ jinantaṁ samupacitasubhaṁ sabbalokeka-
bandhuṁ
nâhu yena pi tulyo kusalamahimato uttamo bhûtaloke
tassevâyaṁ suvimhaṁ suvipulamamalaṁ bodhisam-
bhârabhûtaṁ
hetuṁ hetvânurûpaṁ sugatagataphalaṁ bhâsato me
suṇâtha.

II. Yogâvacarasampattidîpanîgâthâ.

3 Jâto yo navame khaṇe sutadharo sîlena suddhindriyo
saṁsâraṁ bhayato bhavakkhayakaraṁ disvâ sivaṁ
khemato
taṁ sampâpakamaggadesakamuniṁ sampûjayanto tato
buddhânussatibhâvanâdikamato sampâdaye taṁ sivaṁ.

III. Vatthuvisodhanîgâthâ.

4 Buddho ti ko Buddhaguṇo ti ko so
acintayâdittamupâgato yo
anaññasâdhâraṇabhûtamatthaṁ
akâsi kiṁ so kimavoca Buddho.

5 Visuddhakhandhasantâno Buddho ti niyamo kato
khandhasantânasuddhî tu guṇo ti niyamo kato.

6 Akâsi kiccâni dinesu pañca
pasâdayañciddhibalena sena
janânasesaṁ cariyânukûlaṁ
ñatvânavocânusayappahânaṁ.

IV. Anaññasâdhâraṇadîpanîgâthâ.

7 Abbhuggatâ yassa guṇâ anantâ
tibuddhakhettekadivâkaroti
jânâti so lokamimaṁ parañca
sacetanañceva acetanañca
sakassa santânagataṁ paresaṁ
byatîtamappattakamatrabhûtaṁ.

8 Anantasattesu ca lokadhâtusu
ekova sabbe pi samâ na tena
disâsu pubbâdisu cakkavâḷâ
sahassasaṅkhâyapi appameyyâ
ye tesu devâ manujâ ca brahmâ
ekattha saṅgamma hi mantayantâ.

9 Anâdikâlâgatanâmarûpinaṁ
yathâsakaṁ hetuphalattavuttinaṁ
tabbhâvabhâvittamasambhuṇantâ
nânâvipallâsamanupaviṭṭhâ.

10 Kammappavattiñca phalappavattiṁ
ekattanânattanirîhadhammataṁ
viññattisantânaghanena channato
sivañjasaṁ no bhaṇituṁ samatthâ.

11 Eko va so santikaro pabhaṅkaro
saṅkhâya ñeyyâni asesitâni
tesañhi majjhe paramâsambhîvadaṁ
sivañjasaṁ dîpayituṁ samattho.

12 So Gotamo Sakyasuto munindo
sabbassa lokassa padîpabhûto
anantasatte bhavabandhanamhâ
mocesi kâruññaphalânupekkhî.

V. Abhinîhâradîpanîgâthâ.

13 Vadetha tassîdha anappakaṁ guṇaṁ
na tena tulyo paramo ca vijjati
kiṁ taṁ guṇaṁ taṁ sadisena dinnaṁ
sayaṁkataṁ kinnu adhiccaladdhaṁ.

14 Nâdhiccaladdhaṁ na ca pubbabuddhâ
brahmâdinaṁ sammutiyâ bahûnaṁ
sayaṁkateneva anopamena
dânâdinâ laddhamidaṁ vipâkaṁ.

15 Ito catunnaṁ asaṅkhiyânaṁ
sataṁsahassânadhikânamatthake
kappe atîtamhi Sumedhatâpaso
vehâyasaṁ gacchati iddhiyâ tadâ.

16 Dipaṅkaro nâma jino sasaṅgho
Rammaṁ puraṁ yâti virocamâno
manussadevehibhipûjiyanto
sahassaraṁsi viya bhâṇumâ nabhe.

17 Tassañjasaṁ kûtabahussahânaṁ
Buddho ti sutvâ sumano patîto
mamajja dehaṁ panimassa datvâ
Buddho ahaṁ hessamanâgatediso.

18 Tasmiñjase kandaratamhi paṅke
katvâna setuṁ sayi so sadehaṁ
Buddho ayaṁ gacchatu piṭṭhiyâ mamaṁ
bodhissace hessati me anâgate.

19 Ussîsakaṁ yâti jino hi tassa
ajjhâsayo sijjhatimassanâgate
ñatvâna byâkâsi asesato hi
Buddho ayaṁ hessatinâgatesu.

20 Sutvâna patto va mahâbhisekaṁ
laddhaṁ va bodhiṁ samanussaranto
pûjetvâ yâte munidevamânuse
uṭṭhâya so sammasi pâramî dasa.

21 Daḷhaṁ gahetvâ samatiṁsapâramî
sikkhattayañcassa jinassa santike
kâtuṁ samattho pi bhavassa pâraṁ
sattesu kâruññabalâ bhavaṁ gato.

22 Uppannuppannake so jinavaramatule pûjayitvâ asesaṁ
Buddho eso hi poso bhavati niyamato byâkato tehi tehi
tesaṁ tesaṁ jinânaṁ vacanamanupamaṁ pûjayitvâ sirena
taṁ taṁ dukkhaṁ sahitvâ sakalaguṇadadaṁ pâramî pûrayittha.

VI. Bodhisambhâradîpanîgâthâ.

23 So dukkhakhinnajanadassanadukkhakhinno
kâruññameva janatâya akâsi niccaṁ
tesaṁ hi mocanamupâyamidan ti ñatvâ
tâdîparâdhamapi attani ropayî so.

24 Dânâdinekavarapâramisâgaresu
ogâḷhatâya pi paduṭṭhajanena dinnaṁ
dukkhaṁ tathâ atimahantatarampi kiñci
nâññâsi sattahitameva gavesayanto.

25 Chetvâna sîsaṁ hi sakaṁ dadanto
maṁsaṁ pacitvâna sakaṁ dadanto
so cattagatto paṇidhânakâle
duṭṭhassa kiṁ dussati chedanena.

26 Evaṁ anantamapi jâtisatesu dukkhaṁ
patvâna sattahitameva gavesayanto
Dîpaṅkare gahitasîlasamâdhipaññaṁ
pûlesi yâva sakabodhitale suniṭṭho.

27 Yadâbhinîhâramakâ Sumedho
yadâ ca Maddiṁ adadâ Sivindo
etthantare jâtisu kiñcipekaṁ
niratthakaṁ no agamâsi tassa.

28 Mahâsamudde jalabinduto pi
tadantare jâti anappakâ va
nirantaraṁ pûritapâramînaṁ
kathaṁ pamâṇaṁ upamâ kuhiṁ vâ.

29 Yo maggapasse madhurambabîjaṁ
châyâphalatthâya mahâjanânaṁ
ropesi tasmiṁ hi khaṇeva tena
châyâphale puññamaladdhamuddhaṁ.

30 Tatheva saṁsârapathe janânaṁ
hitâya attanamabhiropitakkhaṇe
siddhaṁ va puññûpari tassa tasmiṁ
dhanaṅgajîvaṁ pi haranti ye ye.

31 So sâgare jaladhikaṁ ruhiraṁ adâsi
bhûmâparâjiya samaṁsamadâsi dânaṁ
meruppamâṇamadhikañca samoḷisîsaṁ
khe târakâdhikataraṁ nayanaṁ adâsi.

VII. Gabbhokkantidîpanîgâthâ.

32 Gambhîrapânadânâdisâgaresu hi thâmasâ
taranto Maddidânena niṭṭhâpetvâna pâramî.

33 Vasanto Tusîte kâye bodhiparipâkamâgamma
âyâcanâya ca devânaṁ mâtugabbhamupâgami.

34 Sato ca sampajâno ca mâtukucchimhi okkami
tassa okkantiyaṁ sabbâ dasasahassî pakampittha.

35 Tato pubbanimittâni dvattiṁsâni tadâ siyuṁ
tuṭṭhahaṭṭhâ va sâ mâtâ puttaṁ passati kucchiyaṁ.

VIII. Vijâyanamaṅgaladîpanîgâthâ.

36 Sâ puṇṇagabbhâ dasamâsato paraṁ
gantvâna phullaṁ varalumbinîvanaṁ
ṭhitâ gahetvâ varasâlasâkhaṁ
vijâyi taṁ puttavaraṁ sukhena.

37 Tadâ sahassîdasalokadhâtusu
devâ ca nâgâ asurâ ca yakkhâ
nânâdisâ maṅgalacakkavâḷaṁ
sumaṅgalaṁ maṅgalamâgamiṁsu.

38 Anekasâkhañca sahassamaṇḍalaṁ
chattaṁ marû dhârayumantalikkhe
suvaṇṇadaṇḍâ vipatanti câmarâ
khajjiṁsu bherî ca nadiṁsu saṅkhâ.

39 Malenakenâpi anûpalitto
ṭhito va pâdâni pasârayanto
kathî va dhammâsanatotaranto
jâto yathâdiccavaro nabhamhâ.

40 Khîṇâsavâ brahmagaṇopagantvâ
suvaṇṇajâlena paṭiggahesuṁ
tato ca devâjinacammakena
tato dukûlena ca taṁ manussâ.

41 Tesaṁ pi hatthâ varabhûmiyaṁ ṭhito
disâ vilokesi sabbâ samantato
vadiṁsu devâ pi ca brahmakâyikâ
tayâ samo katthaci natthi uttaro.

42 Gantvâna uttaraṁ satta padavârehi vikkamo
sîhanâdaṁ nadî tesaṁ devatânaṁ hi sâvayaṁ.

43 Tato puttaṁ gahetvâna gatâ mâtâ sakaṅgharaṁ
mâtâ sattamiyaṁ gantvâ devaputtattamâgami.

44 Te brahmaṇâ pañcamiyaṁ subhuttâ
nâmaṁ gahetuṁ varalakkhaṇâni
disvâna ekaṅgulimukkhipiṁsu
buddho ayaṁ hessati vîtarâgo.

45 Jiṇṇañca disvâ byâdhikaṁ matañca
avhâyitaṁ pabbajitañca disvâ
ohâya pabbajjamupeti kâme
Buddho ayaṁ hessati vîtarâgo.

IX. Agâriyasampattidîpanîgâthâ.

46 Kâlakkamena cando va vaḍḍhanto vaḍḍhite kule
puññodayenudento so bhâṇumâ viya ambare.

47 Siddhatthako hi Siddhattho laddhâ deviṁ Yasodharaṁ
cattâlîsasahassehi pûritthîhi purakkhito.

48 Rammasurammasubhesu gharesu
tiṇṇamutûnamanucchavikesu
dibbasukhaṁ viya bhuñji sukhaṁ so
acchariyabbhutarâjavibhûtiṁ.

X. Nekkhammajjhâsayadîpanîyamakagâthâ.

Namo tassa yato mahimato yassa tamo na.

49 Disvâ nimittâni madacchidâni
thînaṁ virûpâni ratacchidâni
pâpâni kammâni sukhacchidâni
laddhâni ñâṇâni bhavacchidâni.

50 Padittagehâ viya bheravaṁ ravaṁ
ravaṁ samuṭṭhâya gato mahesi
mahesimolokiyaputtamattano
tanosi no pemamahoghamattano.

51 Ummâraummâragatuddharitvâ
padaṁ padaṁ yâtanarâsabhassa
alaṁ alaṁkâratarena gantuṁ
matî matîvetimanaṅgabhaṅge.

52 Ummâraummâragato mahesi
anaṅgabhaṅgaṁ samacintayittha
kiṁ me jarâmaccumukhe ṭhitassa
na me vase kâmavase ṭhitassa.

53 Kâmena kâmena na sâdhyamokkhaṁ
mânena mânena mamatthi kiñci
Mâro saseno hi avâraṇîyo
yantena ucchuṁ viya maddatî maṁ.

54 Âdittamuyâtapayâtamûnaṁ
atâṇâleṇâsaraṇe jane te
disvâna disvâna sivaṁ mayâ te
kâmena kâmena kathaṁ vineyya.

55 Vijjâvijjâya cutañcupetaṁ
asârasârûpagatañjanaṁ janaṁ
vijjâyavijjâya yuto cutohaṁ
pahomi târetumasaṅgaho gato.

56 Magganti no diṭṭhigatâpavaggaṁ
aggâ ti tevâhu janâ samaggâ
naggaṁ aho mohatamassa vaggaṁ
vaggaṁ hanissâmi tamaggamaggâ.

57 Paseyhakârena aseyhadukkhaṁ
janâ janentîha janânameva
paseyhakârenâ aseyhadukkhaṁ
pâpaṁ na jânanti tato nidânaṁ.

58 Te oghayogâsavasaṁkilesâ
tameva nâsenti tato samuṭṭhitâ
ekantikaṁ jâti jarâ ca maccu
nirantaraṁ taṁ byasanañcanekaṁ.

59 Cîraṁ kilesânasamujjalantaṁ
disvâna sattânusayaṁ sayambhû
sâdhemi bodhiṁ vinayâmi satte
pacchâ pi passâmi sutaṁ sutantaṁ.

60 Taṁ dibbacakkaṁ khuracakkamâlaṁ
rajjaṁ sasârajjasamajjamajjaṁ
te bandhavâ bandhanamâgatâ pare
suto pasûtoyamanaṅgadûto.

61 Samujjalantaṁ vasatî satîsirî
sirîsapâgâramidaṁ mahâvisaṁ
daddallamânâ yuvatî vatîmâ
sakaṇṭakâyeva samañjasañjase.

62 Yassâ virâjitasirî siriyâ pi natthi
tassâvalokiya na tittivasânamatthi
gacchâmi handa tavanaṅga sirappabhedaṁ
mattebhakumbhupari sîhavilâsagâmiṁ.

63 Bho bho anaṅgasucira pi panuṇṇabâṇa
bâṇâni saṁhara panuṇṇamito nirodha
rodhena câpadagato manaso na soca
socaṁ tavappanavalokiya yâmi santiṁ.

64 Ratî ratî kâmaguṇe viveke
alaṁ alanteva vicintayanto
manaṁ manaṅgâlayasampadâlayaṁ
tahiṁ tahiṁ diṭṭhabâlâ va pakkami.

XI. Pâduddhâravimhayadîpanîgâthâ.

65 Yâvañcayaṁ ravi caratyacalena ruddhe
yâvañca cakkaratanañca payâti loke
tâvissaro nabhacaro jitacâturanto
hitvâ kathaṁ nu padamuddhari so nirâso.

66 Dipe mahâ ca caturâdhikadvesahasse
tatrâpi seṭṭhabhajitaṁ varajambudîpaṁ
bhûnâbhikaṁ Kapilavatthupuraṁ surammaṁ
hitvâ kathaṁ nu padamuddhari so nirâso.

67 Ñâtînasîti kulato hi sahassa Sâkye
hatthissadhaññadhanino vijitârisaṅghe
Gottena Gotamabhavaṁ pitarañjanaggaṁ
hitvâ kathaṁ nu padamuddhari so nirâso.

68 Rammaṁ Surammavasatiṁ ratanujjalantaṁ
gimhe pi vimhayakaraṁ suramandirâbhaṁ
ussâpitaddhajapaṭâkasitâtapattaṁ
hitvâ kathaṁ nu padamuddhari so nirâso.

69 Sapokkharâ pokkharaṇî catasso
supupphitâ mandirato samantâ
kokâ nadantûpari kokanâde
hitvâ kathaṁ nu padamuddhari so nirâso.

70 Sare saroje ruditâḷipâḷi
samantato passati pañjarañjasâ
disvâravindâni mukhâravindaṁ
nâthassa lajjâ viya saṁkujanti.

71 Madhurâ madhurâbhirutâ
caritâ padume padumeḷigaṇâ
vasatiṁ adhunâ madhunâ
akaruṁ jahitaṁ kimidaṁ patinâ.

72 Tamhâ rasaṁ madhukarâ bhavanaṁ haritvâ
ninnâdino samadhuraṁ madhuraṁ karonti
nâdena nâdamatiriccupavîṇayanti
naccanti tâ surapure vaṇitâ va tâva.

73 Sañcoditâ pîṇapayodharâdharâ
virâjitânaṅgajamekhalâkhalâ
suraṅgaṇâ vaṅgajaphassadâ sadâ
ramâ ramâpenti varaṅgadâgadâ.

74 Karâtirattâ ratirattarâmâ
tâḷenti tâḷâvacare samantâ
naccuggatânekasahassahatthâ
Sakko pi kiṁ Sakyasamoti codayuṁ.

75 Visâlanettâ hasulâ sumajjhâ
nimbatthanî vimhayagîtasaddâ
alaṅkatâ malladharâ suvatthâ
naccanti tâḷâvacarehi ghuṭṭhâ.

76 Yâsaṁ hi loke upamâ natthi
tâsaṁ hi phassesu kathâvakâsâ
taṁ tâdisaṁ kâmaratiṁnubhonto
hitvâ kathaṁ nu padamuddhari so nirâso.

77 Pâdepâde valayaviravâmekhalâvîṇânâdâ
gîtaṁgîtaṁ patiratikaraṁ gâyatî gâyatî sâ
hatthehatthe valayacalitâ sambhamaṁ sambhamanti
disvâdisvâ iti ratikaraṁ yâti hâhâ kimhâ.

XII. Apunarâvattigamanadîpanîyamakagâthâ.

78 Anantakâlopacitena tena
puññena nibbattavimânayâne
tasmiṁ dine jâtasutaṁ pajâpatiṁ
hitvâ gato so sugato gato va.

79 Taṁ jîvamânaṁ pitarañca mâtaraṁ
te ñâtake tâdisiyo ca itthiyo
te tâdise rammakare nikete
hitvâ gato so sugato gato va.

80 Khomañca pattuṇṇadukûlacînaṁ
sakâsikaṁ sâdhusugandhavâsitaṁ
nivâsito sobhati vâsavo va
hitvâ gato so sugato gato va.

81 Vidhippakâsâ nidhiyo catasso
samuggatâ bhûtadharâ vasundharâ
sattâvasattâvasudhâ sudhâsâ
hitvâ gato so sugato gato va.

82 Suvaṇṇathâle satarâjike subhe
sâdhuṁ sugandhaṁ sucisâlibhojanaṁ
bhutvâ savâsîhi vilâsinîhi
hitvâ gata so sugato gato va.

83 Manuññagandhena asuññagandho
sugandhagandhena vilittagatto
sugandhavâtena suvijjitaṅgo
hitvâ gato so sugato gato va.

84 Sulakkhaṇe hevabhilakkhitaṅgo
pasâdhito devapasâdhanena
virocamâno samarâjinîhi
hitvâ gato so sugato gato va.

85 Nânâsanâni sayanâni nivesanâni
bhâbhânibhâni ratanâkarasannibhâni
tatrussitâni ratanaddhajabhûsitâni
hitvâ va tâni bimabindusamâni tâni.

86 Nânâvidhehi ratanehi samujjalehi
nârihi niccamupagâyitahamṁiyehi
rajjehi cakkaratanâdivibhûsitehi
yâto tato hi mahito purisassarehi.

XIII. Dvipâdabyâsayamakagâthâ.

87 Yasodharaṁ pîṇapayodharâdharaṁ
anaṅgaraṅgaddhajabhûtamaṅgaṁ
devaccharâvujjalitaṁ patibbataṁ
hitvâ gato so sugato va nûna.

88 Sabbâvanicchandamatiṁ Pabbâvatiṁ
bhatto Kuso saṁhari bhattakâjaṁ
tâyâbhirûpaṁ pi Yasodharaṁ varaṁ
hitvâ gato so sugato va nûna.

89 Pure pure saṇcari khaggahattho
varaṁ paritthînam Anitthigandho
siriñca riñcâpi na riñci nâriṁ
hitvâṇimandâni gato tathâgato.

90 Harittaco râgabalena deviyâ
avatthaliṅgena na liṅganussari
asevi kâmaṁ tamidâni kâmaṁ
hitvâ gato so sugato va nûna.

91 Apameyyakappesu vivekasevî
hitvâ gato rajjasirim varitthiṁ
aṇuṁ kaliṁ vaṇṇayi taṁ purâṇaṁ
vatthambhi chiddaṁ viya tunnakâro.

92 Tathâ ti mantvâna idâninaṅgo
Yasodharaṁ paggahito dhajaṁ va
matto jitomhî ti pamattabandhu
na passi ñâṇûsanipâtamantaraṁ.

93 Disvâna dukkhânalasambhavaṁbhavaṁ
katvâ taduppâdakanaṅgabhaṅgaṁ
Yasodharaṁ pîṇapayodharâdharaṁ
hitvâ gato Buddhabalappadaṁ padaṁ.

94 Anantasattânamanantakâle
manaṅgahetvâna jito anaṅgo
parâjito nûna hi ekakassa
tathâgato so na punâgato va.

95 Disvâna ñâṇâsanipâtamantaraṁ
tathâgato so na punâgato va
Tatbâgato so na punâgato va
disvânañâṇâsanipâtamantaraṁ.

XIV. Tipâdabyâsayamakagâthâ.

96 Tathâgataccheramahosi tassa
tathâ himâropitadâhasantiṁ
tathâ hi Mâro pi tadâha santiṁ
tathâ hi mâropi tadâ hasantiṁ.

XV. Pâdabyâsamahâyamakagâthâ.

97 Sakâmadâtâ vinayâmanantagû
sakâmadâtâ vinayâmanantagû
sakâmadâtâ vinayâmanantagû
sakâmadâtâ vinayâmanantagû.

XVI. Abyâpetâdyantayamakagâthâ.

98 Raveraverorabhimârabherave
raveraverereriva bherave rave
rave rave sûditagârave rave
raveravedesi jinorave rave.

XVII. Paṭilomayamakagâthâ.

99 Lokâyâtatayâ kâlo visesaṁ na na saṁsevi
visesaṁ na na saṁsevi lokâ yâtatayâ kâlo.

100 Râjarâjayasopetavisesaṁ racitaṁ mayâ
yâmataṁ cirasaṁsevitapeso yajarâjarâ.

XVIII. Ekaṭhânikâdiyamakagâthâ.

101 Âkaṅkhakkhâkaṅkhaṅga kaṅkhâgaṅgâkhâgahaka
kaṅkhâgâhakakaṅkhâgha hâ hâ kaṅkhâ kahaṁ
kahaṁ.

102 Apagabbho apagabbho amoho mâ pamohako
maggamukhaṁ mokhamâha mâhâ mohamûhak-
khamaṁ.

103 Pâpâpâpabhavaṁ passaṁ pâpâpâpabhavuggato
pâpâpâpabhavâsaṅgâ pâpâpâpabhavâgato.

104 Kusalâkusalaṁ passaṁ kusalâkusalaṁ caji
kusalâkusalâsaṅgâ kusalâkusalâ cuto.

XIX. Akkharuttarikayamakagâthâ.

105 Nonânino nanûnâni nanenâni nanânino
nunnânenâni nûna na nânanaṁ nânanena no.

106 Sâro surâsure sârî rasasârasarissaro
rasasârarase sârî surâsurasarassire.

107 Devânaṁ nandano devo devadeve na nandi no
vedadînena vedena vedi vedena vedino.

108 Devâsane nisinno so devadevo sasâsane
nisinnânaṁ sadevânaṁ desesi dassanâsanaṁ.

XX. Paheḷigâthâ.

109 Dasanâvagato sañño andhassa tamado ravi
aṭṭhamâpuṇṇasaṅkappo pâtvanaññamanaññiva.

XXI. Byâpetâdiyamakagâthâ.

110 Ekantameva saparatthaparo mahesi
ekantameva dasapâramitâbalena
ekantameva hatamârabalena tena
ekantameva suvisuddhamalattha bodhiṃ.

XXII. Mahâpadhânadîpanîgâthâ.

111 Orohitorohitapâpadhammo
channena sa Channahayena gantvâ
Anomatîramhi anomasatto
anomapabbajjamupâgato so.

112 Nirâmisaṁ pîtisukhaṁ anûpamaṁ
Anûpiye ambavane alattha
sarûpasobhâya virûpasobhaṁ
sarâjikaṁ Râjagahaṁ karittha.

113 Tato Aḷâr Ûdakatâpasânaṁ
jhânenasantuṭṭhamano vihâya
mahâpadhânây Uruvelabhûmiṁ
gato sikhappattamakâsi dukkaraṁ.

114 Na kâmato nevatidukkaramhi
sabbaññutâ sijjhati majjhimâya
ñatvâna taṁ pubbaguṇopaladdhaṁ
dhammaṁ samânetumagâ subodhiṁ.

XXIII. Mâraparâjayadîpanîgâthâ.

115 Tibuddhakhettambhi tisetachattaṁ
laddhâna lokâdhipatî bhaveyya
gantvâna bodhimhiparâjitâsane
yuddhâya mârenacalo nisîdi.

116 Datvâna maṁsaṁ rajjaṁ pitâ Suddhodano tadâ
namassamâno sirasâ setachattena pûjayi.

117 Sahampati Mahâbrahmâ devabrahmehi ekato
attano visaye rajjaṁ datvâna chattena pûjayi.

118 Sayaṁ Nârâyanabalo abhiññâbalapâragû
jetuṁ sabbassa lokassa bodhimaṇḍamupâgami.

119 Tadâ Vasavattîrâjâ chakâmavacarissaro
sasenâvâhano bodhimaṇḍaṁ yuddhâyupâgami.

120 Etha gaṇhatha bandhatha chaṭṭetha ceṭakaṁ imaṃ
manussakalale jâto kimihanti na maññati.

121 Jalantaṁ navavidhaṁ vassaṁ vassâpeti anappakaṁ
dhûmandhakâraṁ katvâna pâtesi asinaṁ bahuṁ.

122 Cakkâvudhaṁ khipento pi nâsakkhi kiñci kâtave
gahetabbaṁ hi gahaṇaṁ apassanto itibravi.

123 Siddhattha kasmâ âsi nu âsane mama santake
uṭṭhehi âsanâ no ce phâlemi hadayaṁ tava.

124 Sapâdamûle kîḷantaṁ passanto taruṇaṁ sutaṁ
pitâ vudikkhi taṁ Mâraṁ mettâyanto dayaparo.

125 Tadâ so asambhivâcaṁ sīhanâdaṁ nadî Muni
na jânâti sayaṁ mayhaṁ dâsabhâvapiyaṁ khaḷo.

126 Yena kenaci kammena jâto devapure vare
sakaṁ gatiṁ ajânanto lokajeṭṭhoti maññati.

127 Anantalokadhâtumhi sattânaṁ hi kataṁ subhaṁ
mayhekapâramiyâ pi kalaṁ nagghati soḷasiṁ.

128 Tiracchâno saso hutvâ disvâ yâcakamâgataṁ
pacitvâna sakaṁ maṁsaṁ patitoggimhi dâtave.

129 Evaṁ anantakâlesu kataṁ dukkarakârikaṁ
ko hi nâma kareyyañño anummatto sacetano.

130 Evaṁ anantapuññehi siddhaṁ dehamimaṁ pana
yathâbhûtaṁ ajânanto manussosî ti maññati.

131 Nâhaṁ manussomanusso na brahmâ na ca devatâ
jarâmaraṇaṁ lokassa dassetuṁ panidhâgato.

132 Anupalitto lokena jâtonantajino ahaṁ
buddho bodhitale hutvâ târemi janataṁ bahuṁ.

133 Samantâ dhajinaṁ disvâ yuddhaṁ Mâraṁ savâhanaṁ
yuddhâya paccugacchâmi mâ maṁ ṭhânâ acâvayi.

134 Yante taṁ nappasahati senaṁ loko sadevako
tante paññâya gacchâmi âmaṁ pattaṁ va asmanâ.

135 Icchanto sâsape gabbhe caṅkamâmi ito cito
icchanto lokadhâtumhi attabhâvena châdayi.

136 Ete sabbe gahetvâna cuṇṇetuṁ accharâya pi
atthi thâmaṁ balaṁ mayhaṁ pâṇaghâto na vaṭṭati.

137 Imassa gaṇḍuppâdassa âyudhena balena kiṁ
mayhaṁ hi tena pâpena sallâpo pi na yujjati.

138 Pallaṅkaṁ mama bhâvâya kimatthaññena sakkhinâ
kampitâ Maddiyâ dânâ sakkhi hoti ayaṁ mahî.

139 Iti vatvâ dakkhiṇaṁ bâhuṁ pathaviyâ paṇâmayi
tadâ kampittha pathavî mahâghoso ajâyatha.

140 Pathavîghosena âkâse gajjanto asani phali
tasmiṁ majjhe gato Mâro sapariso bhayatajjito.

141 Mahâvâtasamuddhatabhasmaṁ va vikiriyyatha
mahâghoso ajâyittha Siddhatthassa jayo iti.

XXIV. Abhisambodhidîpanîgâthâ.

142 Purato gacchati cando rajatacakkaṁ va ambare
sahassaraṁsi sûriyo pacchimenupagacchati.

143 Majjhe bodhidumacchatte pallaṅke apparâjite
pallaṅkena nisîditvâ dhammaṁ sammasate Muni.

144 Sakko tasmiṁ khaṇe saṅkhaṁ dhamanto abhidhâvati
Brahmâ tiyojanaṁ chattaṁ dhâreti Munimuddhani.

145 Maṇitâlavaṇṭaṁ Tusito Suyâmo vâḷabîjaniṁ
nânâmaṅgalabhaṇḍâni gahito sesadevatâ.

146 Evaṁ dasasahassamhi Sakko Brahmâ ca devatâ
saṅkhâdîni dhamantâ ca cakkavâḷamhi pûrayuṁ.

147 Maṅgalâni gahetvâna tiṭṭhanti kâci devatâ
dhajamâlâ gahetvâna tathâ puṇṇaghaṭâdayo.

148 Tattha naccanti gâyanti seḷenti vâdayanti ca
devâ dasasahassamhi tuṭṭhahaṭṭhâ pamoditâ.

149 Dhammâmatarasassâdaṁ labhissâmassa santike
nayanâmatarasassâdaṁ pâṭihâriyañca passituṁ.

150 Jâramaraṇakantârâ sokopâyâsasallato
mocesi kâmapâsamhâ desento amataṁ padaṁ.

151 Iti tuṭṭhehi devehi pûjiyanto narâsabho
kiñci pûjaṁ acintento cintento dhammamuttamaṁ.

152 Sabbatthasâdhito santo Siddhattho apparâjito
cakkavâḷasilâsâṇipâkârehi manorame.

153 Târâmaṇikhacitâkâsavitâne candadîpake
mânâratanapajjote mâlâgandhâdipûjite.

154 Dibbehi chaṇabherîhi ghuṭṭhe maṅgalagîtiyâ
cakkavâḷe supâsâde bodhimaṇḍamahâtale.

155 Bodhirukkhamaṇicchatte pallaṅke apparâjito
nisinno paṭhame yâme purimaṁ jâtimanussari.

156 Nâmarûpânamuppatti sudiṭṭhâ hoti tenidhâ
sakkâyadiṭṭhi tenassa pahînâ hoti sabbaso.

157 Tato hi dutiye yâme yathâkammupage sari
sudiṭṭhaṁ hoti tenassa kammakkilesehi sambhavaṁ.

158 Kaṅkhâvitaraṇî nâma ñâṇantaṁ samupâgataṁ
tenasesa pahîyittha kaṅkhâ soḷasadhâ ṭhitâ.

159 Tato so tatiye yâme dvâdasaṅge asesato
so paṭiccasamuppâde ñâṇamotârayî Muni.

160 Avijjavâdyânulomena jarâdipaṭilomato
sammasanto yathâbhûtaṁ ñâṇadassanamâgami.

161 Kappakoṭisatenâpi appameyyesu jâtisu
lobhaṁ asesadânena vinâsento puṇappunaṁ.

162 Sîlena khantimettâya kodhadosaṁ nivâresi
paññâya mohaṁ chetvâna micchâdiṭṭhi tatheva ca.

163 Garûpasevanâdîhi vicikicchaṁ vinodayaṁ
mânuddhaccaṁ vinodento kule jeṭṭhopacâyinâ.

164 Nekkhammena vinâsento kâmarâgaṁ punappunaṁ
saccena visaṁvâdaṁ kosajjaṁ vîriyena ca.

165 Evaṁ dânâdinâ taṁ taṁ kilesaṅgaṁ vinodayaṁ
suvaḍḍhitâ mahâpaññâ kathaṁ santiṁ na rûhati.

166 Sudukkaraṁ karitvâna dânâdipaccayaṁ pure
na kiñci bhavasampattiṁ patthesi bodhimuttamaṁ.

167 Paṇidhânamhâ paṭṭhâya kataṁ puññañca patthanaṁ
ekattha dâni sampattiṁ deti bodhiṁ asaṁsayaṁ.

168 Tato so sabbasaṅkhâre aniccadukkhanattato
sammasantonulomena nibbânaṁ samupâgami.

169 Savâsane kilese so jhâpentonumattaṁ pi ca
arahattappattiyâ suddho Buddho bodhitale ahu.

170 Patto vimuttiṁ varasetachattaṁ
so pîtivegena udânudîrayi
chetvâna Mâre vijitârisaṅgho
tibuddhakhettekadivâkaro ahu.

171 Râjâdhirâjâ varamevamâsi
tichattadhârî varadhammarâjâ
mahâsahassaṁ pi ca lokadhâtuṁ
sarena viññâpayituṁ samattho.

172 Buddho lokâloke loke
jâto satto konummatto
suddhaṁ buddhaṁ oghâ tiṇṇaṁ
saddho pañño ko no vande.

173 Bhajitaṁ cajitaṁ pavanaṁ bhavanaṁ
jahitaṁ gahitaṁ samalaṁ amalaṁ
sugataṁ agataṁ sugatiṁ agatiṁ
namitaṁ amitaṁ namatiṁ sumatim.

XXV. Dhammacakkapavattanadîpanîgâthâ.

174 Sammâsambodhiñânaṁ hatasakalamalaṁ suddhato cûtisuddhaṁ
addhâ laddhâ suladdhaṁ vatamiti satataṁ cintayanto subodhiṁ
sattâhaṁ sattamevaṁ vividhaphalasukhaṁ vitinâmesi kâlaṁ
Brahmenâyâcito so Isipatanavane vattayî dhammacakkaṁ.

XXVI. Pâṭihâriyadîpanîgâthâ.

175 Brahmassa saddaṁ karavîkabhâṇiṁ
yathicchitaṁ sâvayituṁ samatthaṁ
saccaṁ piyaṁ bhûtahitaṁ vadantaṁ
na pûjaye ko hi naro sacetano.

176 Iddhi ca âdesanânusâsanî
pâṭihîre Bhagavâ vasî ahu
katvâna accherasupâṭihîraṁ
desesi dhammaṁ anukampimaṁ pajaṁ.

XXVII. Navaguṇadîpanîgâthâ.

177 Evaṁ hi buddhattamupâgato so
desesi dhammaṁ sanarâmarânaṁ
nânânayehîbhisamesi satte
tasmâ hi jhâto tibhavesu nâtho.

178 Addhâ laddhâ dhammâlokaṁ
diṭṭhâ pattâ ñâtâ saccaṁ
tiṇṇârâgâdosamohâ
thomesuṁ te devâ brahmâ.

179 Munirâjavaro nararâjavaro
dividevavaro sucibrahmavaro
sakapâpaharo parapâpaharo.
sakavuḍḍhikaro paravuḍḍhikaro.

180 Sanarâmarubrahmagaṇebhi rutâ
arahâdiguṇâ vipulâ vimalâ
navadhâ vasudhâgagaṇe gahaṇâ
sakale tidive tibhave visaṭâ.

181 Ye pissa te bhagavato ca acintiyâdî
suddhâtisuddhatarabuddhaguṇâ hi sabbe.
saṅkhepato navavidhesu padesu khitâ
vakkhâmi dâni arahâdiguṇe ahaṁ pi.

182 Yo cîdha jâto arahaṁ nirâso
sammâbhisambuddhasamantacakkhu
sampannavijjâcaraṇoghatiṇṇo
sammâgato so sugato gato va.

183 Avedi so lokamimaṁ parañca
anuttaro sârathidammasatte
sadevakânaṁ varasatthukiccaṁ
akâsi buddho bhagavâ visuddho.

XXVIII. Guṇadîpanigâthâ.

184 Na tassa adiṭṭhanamidhatthi kiñci
ato aviññâtamajânitabbaṁ
sabbaṁ abhiññâsi yadatthi ñeyyaṁ
Tathâgato tena samantacakkhu.

185 Iti mahitamanantâkittisambhârasâraṁ
sakaladasasahassîlokadhâtumhi niccaṁ
upacitasubhahetupayutânantakâlaṁ
tadiha sugatabodhisâdhukaṁ cintanîyaṁ.

186 Takkabyâkaraṇañca dhammavinayaṁ sutvâ pi yo paññavâ
tenâyaṁ sucisârabhûtavacanaṁ viññâyate kevalaṁ
hetuñcâpi phalena tena saphalaṁ sampassamâno tato
bodhiṁ saddahateva tassa mahatâvâyamato sambhavaṁ.

187 Yo saddahanto pana tassa bodhiṁ
vuttânusârena guṇerahâdî
katheti cintenti ca so muhuttaṁ
ohâya pâpâni upeti santiṁ.

188 Saddheyyâ te cinteyyâ te
vandeyyâ te pûjeyyâ te
buddholokâloke loke
jâte netaṁ patthentena.

XXIX. Pûjâvidhânadîpanîgâthâ.

189 Tasmâ hi jâtovarakamhi tassa
âyattake maṅgalacakkavâḷe
bhûtehi vatthûhi manoramehi
pûjemi taṁ pûjitpûjitaṁ pure.

190 Sohaṁ ajja panetasmiṁ cakkavâḷamhi pupphite
thalaje jalaje vâ pi sugandhe ca agandhake.

191 Manussesu anekattha taḷâkuyyânavâpisu
pavane Himavantasmiṁ tattha satta mahâsare.

192 Parittadîpe dvisahasse mahâdîpe supupphite
sattaparibhaṇḍaselesu Sinerupabbatuttame.

193 Kumuduppalakâdîni nâgânaṁ bhavanesu pi
pâṭalâdîni pupphâni asurânaṁ hi âlaye.

194 Koviḷârâdikâni tu devatânaṁ hi âlaye
evamâdî anekattha pupphite dharaṇîruhe.

195 Campakâ salalâ nimbâ nâgapunnâgaketakâ
vassikâ mallikâ sâlâ koviḷârâ ca pâṭali.

196 Indîvarâ asokâ ca kaṇikârâ ca makulâ
padumâ puṇḍarikâ ca sogandhikumuduppalâ.

197 Ete caññe ca rukkhâ ca valliyo câpi pupphitâ
sugandhâ sukhasamphassâ nânâvaṇṇanibhâ subhâ.

198 Vicitrâ nîlânekâni pîtâ lohitakâni ca
kâḷâ setâ ca mañjaṭṭha nekavaṇṇâ supupphitâ.

199 Sobhate pabbate heṭṭhâ sarehi vanarâjihi
sandamânâhi gaṅgâhi Himavâ ratanâkaro.

200 Pattakiñjakkhareṇûhi okiṇṇaṁ hoti taṁ vanaṁ
bhamarâ pupphagandhehi samantâ abhinâditâ.

201 Athettha sakuṇâ santi dijâ mañjussarâ subhâ
kûjantamupakûjanti utusaṁpupphite dume.

202 Niccharânaṁ nipâtena pabbatâ abhinâditâ
pañcaṅgikâni tûriyâni dibbâni viya suyyare.

203 Tattha naccanti gâyanti seḷenti vâdayanti ca
accharâ viya devesu kinnarâ samalaṅkatâ.

204 Suvaṇṇapabbatâ tasmiṁ jalantaggisikhûpamâ
tasmiṁ hi kinnarâ kiccaṁ padîpena karîyati.

205 Muttâjâlâva dissanti niccharânaṁ hi pâtakâ
pajjalantâ va tiṭṭhanti maṇiveḷuriyâdayo.

206 Kâḷânusâri taggaraṁ kappûraṃ haricandanaṁ
sakuṇânaṁ hi saddena mayûrânaṁ hi kekayâ.

207 Bhamarânaṁ hi ninnâdâ koñcanâdena hatthinaṁ
vijambhitena vâḷânaṁ kinnarânaṁ hi gîtiyâ.

208 Pabbatânaṁ hi obhâsâ maṇinaṁ jotiyâ pi ca
vicitrabbhavitânehi dumânaṁ pupphadhûpiyâ
evaṁ sabbaṅgasampannaṁ kiṁ siyâ Nandanaṁ
vanaṁ.

209 Evaṁ susamphullavanaṁ hi yaṁ yaṁ
tahiṁ tahiṁ pupphitapupphitaṁ subhaṁ
mâlaṁ susaddañca manuññagandhaṁ
pûjemi taṁ pûjitapûjitaṁ purâ.

210 Nâgaloke manusse ca deve brahme ca yaṁ siyâ
sâmuddikaṁ bhûmigataṁ âkâsaṭṭhañca yaṁ dhanaṁ.

211 Rajataṁ jâtarûpañca muttâ veḷuriyâ maṇi
masâragallaṁ phalikaṁ lohitaṅgaṁ pavâḷakaṁ.

212 Yo so anantakappesu pûretvâ dasapâramî
Buddho bodhesi sattânaṁ tassa pûjemi taṁ dhanaṁ.

213 Khomaṁ koseyyaṁ kappâsaṁ sâṇaṁ bhaṅgañca
kambalaṁ
dukûlâni ca dibbâni dussâni vividhâni te.

214 Anantavatthadânena hirottappâdisaṁvaraṁ
yassa siddhaṁ siyâ tassa dussâni pujayâmahaṁ.

215 Pavane jâtarukkhânaṁ nânâphalarasuttamaṁ
ambâ kapiṭṭhâ panasâ cocamocâdinappakâ.

216 Tasmiṁ gandharasaṁ ojaṁ buddhaseṭṭhassa pûjitaṁ
vandâmi sirasâ niccaṁ vippasannena cetasâ.

217 Pûjemi paṭhamaṁ tassa paṇidhânaṁ acintiyaṁ
cakkavâḷamhi sabbehi vijjamânehi vatthuhi.

218 Dasannaṁ pâramînantu pûritaṭṭhânamuttamaṁ
tato sâlavane ramme jâtaṭṭhânaṁ carimakaṁ.

219 Chabbasâni padhânasmiṁ karaṇaṁ dukkarakârikaṁ
apparâjitapallaṅkaṁ buddhaṁ Buddhaguṇaṁ name.

220 Cuddasa buddhañâṇâni aṭṭhârasa âveṇikaṁ
pûjemi dasabalañâṇaṁ catuvesârajjamuttamaṁ.

221 Âsayânusayañâṇaṁ indriyânaṁ paroparaṁ
yamakapâṭihîrañca ñâṇaṁ sabbaññutaṁ pi ca.

222 Mahâkaruṇâpattiñâṇaṁ anâvaraṇamiti ca
cha asâdhâraṇânete ñatvâna pûjayâmahaṁ.

223 Tato ca sattasattâhe dhammasammasitaṁ name
Brahmunâ yâcitaṭṭhânaṁ dhammaṁ desayituṁ varaṁ.

224 Isipatane Migadâye dhammacakkapavattanaṁ
tato Veḷuvanârâme vasitaṭṭhânañca pûjaye.

225 Tato Jetavanaṁ rammaṁ ciravutthaṁ mahesinâ
asâdhâraṇamaññesaṁ yamakapâṭihâriyaṁ.

226 Pâricchattakamûlamhi abhidhammañca desanaṁ
Saṅkassanagaradvâre devorohaṇakaṁ pi ca.

227 Tato ca Himavantasmiṁ Mahâsamayadesanaṁ
vuttânetâni ṭhânâni natvâna pujayâmahaṁ.

228 Caturâsîtisahassehi dhammakkhandhehi saṅgahaṁ
piṭakattayaṁ yathâvuttavidhinâ pûjayâmahaṁ.

229 Mârassa attano âyusaṅkhârosajjanaṁ name
Kusinârâya Mallânaṁ yamakasâlamantare.

230 Paṇidhânamhi paṭṭhâya kataṁ kiccaṁ asesato
niṭṭhapetvâna so sabbaṁ parinibbâyinâsavo.

231 Evaṁ nibbâyamânassa katakiccassa tâdino
ciragatâ mahâkaruṇâ na nibbâyittha kiñci pi.

232 Svâyaṁ dhammo vinayo ca desito sâdhukaṁ mayâ
mamaccayena so satthâ dhâtu câpi sarîrajâ.

233 Apparâjitapallaṅkaṁ bodhirukkhañca uttamaṁ
mamaccayena satthâ ti anujâni Mahâmuni.

234 Mama ṭhâne ṭhapetvâna dhâtubodhiñca pûjitaṁ
anujânâmi tumhâkaṁ sâdhanatthaṁ sivañjasaṁ.

235 Tasmâ hi tassa saddhammaṁ uggaṇhitvâ yathâtathaṁ
yo deseti sambuddho ti natvâna pûjayâmahaṁ.

236 Tasmâ sâsapamattaṁ pi jinadhâtuṁ asesiya
vitthinnacakkavâḷamhi natvâna pûjayâmahaṁ.

237 Paramparâbhatânaṁ hi imamhâ boddhirukkhato
sabbesaṁ bodhirukkhânaṁ natvâna pûjayâmahaṁ.

238 Yaṁ yaṁ paribhuñji Bhagavâ pattacîvaramâdikaṁ
sabbaṁ paribhogadhâtuṁ natvâna pûjayâmahaṁ.

239 Yattha katthaci sayito âsinno caṅkame pi vâ
pâdalañchanakaṁ katvâ ṭhito natvâna pûjaye.

240 Na sañjânanti ye Buddhaṁ evarûpo ti ñâtave
kataṁ taṁ paṭimaṁ sabbaṁ natvâna pûjayâmahaṁ.

241 Evaṁ Buddhañca dhammañca saṅghañca anuttaraṁ
cakkavâḷamhi sabbehi vatthûhi pûjayâmahaṁ.

XXX. Patthanâdîpanîgâthâ.

242 Asmiṁ ca pubbe pi ca attabhâve
sabbehi puññehi mayâ katehi
pûjâvidhânehi ca saññamehi
bhave bhave pemaniyo bhaveyyaṁ.

243 Saddhâ hirottappabahussutattaṁ
parakkamo ceva satissamâdhi
nibbedhabhâgî vajirûpamâti-
paññâ ca me sijjhatu yâva bodhiṁ.

244 Râgañca dosañca pahâya mohaṁ
diṭṭhiñca mânaṁ vicikicchitañca
maccheraissâmalavippahîno
anuddhato accapalo bhaveyyaṁ.

245 Bhaveyyahaṁ kenaci nappaseyho
bhogo ca dinnehi paṭehi anomo
bhogo ca kâyo ca mamesa laddho
parûpakârâya bhaveyyaṁ nûna.

246 Dhammena mâtâpitaro bhareyyaṁ
vuḍḍhapacâyî ca bahûpakârî
ñâtîsu mittesu sapattakesu
vuḍḍhiṁ kareyyaṁ hitamattano ca.

247 Metteyyanâthaṁ upasaṅkamitvâ
tassattabhâvaṁ abhipûjayitvâ
laddhâna Veyyâkaraṇaṁ anûnaṁ
Buddho ayaṁ hessatinâgatesu.

248 Lokena kenâpi anûpalitto
dâne rato sîlaguṇe susaṇṭhito
nekkhammabhâgî varañâṇalâbhî
bhaveyyahaṁ thâmabalûpapanno.

249 Sîsaṁ samaṁsaṁ mama hatthapâde
saṁchindamâne pi kareyyakhantiṁ
sacce ṭhito kûtamadhiṭṭhite va
mettâyupekkhâya yuto bhaveyyaṁ.

250 Mahâpariccâgaṁ katvâ pañca
sambodhimaggaṁ avirûdhayanto
chetvâ kilese jitapañcamâro
Buddho bhavissâmi anâgatesu.

NOTES

(1) l. 3. Bodhiṁ = catumaggañâṇaṁ.

Sakalaguṇadadaṁ.] This is explained by "chaḷâbhiññâ cha asâdhâraṇañâṇâni aṭṭharasa âveṇikadhammâ evamâdisakalaguṇadâyakaṁ."

l. 4. Mocayittha = mocesi.

(2) l. 1. Natvâna] from √nam, "to bow," is explained by sakkaccaṁ vanditvâ.

Jinantaṁ = jinaṁ + taṁ. The gloss says "Khandakilesâbhisaṅkhâramaccudevaputtasaṅkhâte pañca mâre jitavâ ti jino."

l. 3. Suvimhaṁ = ativimhaṁ = atiacchariyaṁ = atiabbhutaṁ = ativimhaniyaṁ [*Sk.* suvismya].

l. 4. Hetuṁ.] This refers to the accomplishment of the *Pâramis.*

Me.] The Burmese *Nissaya* makes *me* refer to Buddhadatta through some misapprehension.

N.B.—The first and second stanzas are Saddharâ of twenty-one syllables in each quarter-verse, according to the following scheme :—

– – – | – ⏑ – | – ⏑ ⏑ | ⏑ ⏑ ⏑ | ⏑ – – | ⏑ – – | ⏑ – –

(3) l. 1. *Navame khaṇe.*] This refers to the time when a Buddha comes into existence and teaches the true law. *Gulatthadîpanî* remarks on *jâto navame khaṇe* as follows :—"Nirayapetatiracchânaarûpâsaññasattapaccantimajanapadapañcindriyânaṁ vekallaṁ micchâdiṭṭhi ti aṭṭhakkhaṇe vinimutto navame Buddhuppâdakkhaṇe vattamâne; *yo jâto* ti manussaloke paṭirûpadese uppanno yo yâdiso saddhâvanto ca sammâdiṭṭhiko ca âcârakulaputto." The *Ṭîkâ* has :—"Aṭṭhakkhaṇâ nâma ti tayo apâyâ arûpâ'saññapaccantimampi ca pañcindriyânaṁ vekallaṁ micchâdiṭṭhi ca dâruṇâ; ime aṭṭhakkhaṇâ kusalakiriyâya asamâyâ anokasâ tesaṁ vipariyâyena aṭṭhakkhaṇâ ti veditabbo apâyârûpâsaññapaccantimadesesu uppattito muñcitvâ paripuṇṇindriyo hutvâ Buddhuppâdapaṭimaṇḍite paṭirûpadese uppajjitvâ sammâdiṭṭhiyâ patiṭṭhitabhâvo paramadullabho." The *Ṭîkâ* then refers to the "Kâṇakacchapopamasuttaṁ," and quotes the following scriptural stanza :—

Buddho ca dullabho loke saddhammasavanampi ca
saṅgho ca dullabho loke sappuriso atidullabho
dullabhañca manussataṁ Buddhuppâdo ca dullabho
dullabhâ khaṇasampatti saddhammo paramadullabho.

Khaṇasampatti in this stanza is the *navamakhaṇa* of our text.

(3) l. 4. Buddhânussatibhâvanâdi = The meditation bringing Buddha to mind in the formula "*Iti pi so Bhagavâ araham*," &c., as well as the other *kammaṭṭhânas* leading to *Vipassanâñâṇa*.

Kamato] "successively" = paṭipâṭiyâ [Sk. *kramaśas*].

Sampâdaye tvaṁ sivaṁ = taṁ bhavakkhayakaraṁ nibbânaṁ sâdheyya.

N.B.—The third stanza is *saddalavikkîḷitâ*, the scheme of which for each pâda is :—

- - - | ⏑ ⏑ - | ⏑ - ⏑ | ⏑ ⏑ - | - - ⏑ | - - ⏑ | -

(4) l. 2. Acintiyâdittaṁ = acintiyâdibhâvaṁ = avediyatulaavûciyaavbhâciyabhâvaṁ. The commentator says, "Buddhaguṇo ti ko so ti imassa pañhassa atthe saṁvaṇṇiyamâne sakalaṁ piṭakattayaṁ nappahoti."

(5) l. 1. Visuddhakhandasantâno.] Having the five khandhas in perfect purity. Santâno is explained by *santati*, "existence." "Savâsanasakalakilese niravasesaṁ jhâpetvâ visuddhiñâṇavantattâ visuddhirûpârûpasantatisamudâyo."—*Guḷatthadîpanî*.

l. 2. Niyamo kato.] Literally "discrimination made."

l. 3. Khandhasantânasuddhi.] "Tassa khandhasantânassa guṇiyattâ pakâsiyattâ pâkaṭakamṇattâ guṇo niyamo kato."—*Guḷatthadîpanî*. "Yo anaññasâdhârano saviññattiko sapâṭihâriyo rûpakâyadhammakâyasantatisamudâyo, so Buddho ti niyamo kato."—*Ṭîkâ*. The stanza on the top of page 64 of *Buddhaghosuppatti*, which presented some difficulty when I was translating it, should be interpreted in the light of the explanations of stanza 5 of *Jinâlaṅkâra*.

(6) l. 1. Kiccâni.] The *Pañca kiccâni* are :—

(*a*) Purebhattakiccaṁ—Going on begging rounds before meal.

(*b*) Pacchâbhattak°—Giving instruction to the assembled laity after meal.

(*c*) Pureyâmabhattak°—Instructing the priesthood in the first watch of night.

(*d*) Majjhimayâmabhattak°—Answering questions put by devas in the middle watch.

(*e*) Pacchimayâmabhattak°—Viewing the general affairs of the world with the eye of wisdom in the third watch.

Dinesu = dine dine.

l. 2. Pasâdayañciddhibalena = pasâdayaṁ + ca + iddhibalena.

l. 3. Jinânasesaṁ = jinânaṁ + asesaṁ.

l. 4. Anusaya.] The reading *anussaya* also occurs. The *Seven Anusayas* or *Attachments* are referred to. Ñatvânâvoca = ñatvâna + avoca.

(7) l. 2. Tibuddhakhetta.] Tiṇi Buddhakhettâni nâma *jâtikhettaṁ*, *âṇakhettaṁ*, *visayakhettaṁ*.

l. 6. Byatîtaṁ = bhutvâpagataṁ. The reading vyâtîtaṁ is also met with.

(9) l. 3. Sambhunantā.] This represents the *present participle* of a verb *sambhunāti* (Fourth Conjugation) from the root "bhu," *to know.* This root occurs in the epithet *sayambhu*, "knowing of oneself." The *Ṭīkā* explains *asambhunantā* by "ñāṇena apāpuṇantā, jānituṃ asakkonto." In Sanskrit the causal of √bhu occurs in the sense of "know," while in Pāli the P.P.P. *bhāvita* signifies "known," "understood."

l. 4. Vipallāsa.] The literal meaning of the word is "reversal," "contrariety." The *Dvādasavipallāsaṃ* or *Twelve Contrary Views* referred to are:—

(1) Considering *Impermanent* as *Permanent*.
(2) ,, *Unhappiness* as *Happiness*.
(3) ,, *Bad* as *Good*.
and (4) ,, *Non-individuality* as *Individuality*, each in relation to (a) *saññā*, (b) *citta*, *and* (c) *diṭṭhi*.

(10) l. 3. Viññatti.] Here the two aspects *kāyaviññatti* and *vaciviññatti* are implied.

l. 4. Sivañjasaṃ = Nibbānagāmimaggaṃ.

(11) l. 3. Paramāsambhivadaṃ = uttamaṃ vesārajjappattaasabhivācaṃ. Asabhivācaṃ = asambhitavacanaṃ. Asambhi, "without fear," "tranquillizing."

(12) l. 4. Anupekkhī = anupekkhamāno, explained by "sakkāra garukārādiṃ apekkhamāno." My *Shwe Dagon* copy reads anapekkhī. Instead of *kāruññaphala*, *kāruññabala* is also met.

(13) l. 1. Tassidha = tassa + idha.

l. 3. Sadisena = sadisena Buddhena.

l. 4. Adhiccaladdhaṃ = yathāsambhavena laddhaṃ = akāraṇena laddhaṃ.

(15) l. 1. Ito = imasmā bhaddakappamhā.

Catunnaṃ.] "Dīpaṅkarakoṇḍaññānamantare ekamasaṅkhyeyyaṃ, Koṇḍañña-Maṅgalānamantare ekaṃ, Sobhita-Anomadassīnamantare ekaṃ, Nārada-Padumuttarānamantare ekan ti evaṃ Buddhantaravasena catubbidhānaṃ."

(17) l. 3. Panimassa = pana + imassa.

(18) l. 2. Sayi.] "Lying."

l. 4. Bodhisacce = bodhi + sacce. The metre requires the second syllable to be long. The reading *bodhimsacce* also occurs.

(22) l. 2. Bhavati.] "Bhavati ti vattamānavacanaṃ tasmiṃ khaṇe bhavitabban viya ekantabhāvibhāvadassanattaṃ vuttaṃ."

(23) l. 4. Tādiparādhamapi = Tādi + aparādhaṃ + api. Aparādho = doso.

(26) l. 3. *Samādhi*.] "Self-concentration" by devotion to the *Saṅkhitasikkhattayaṃ*.

(27) l. 1. Yadābhinihāramakā = yadā + abhinihāraṃ + akā (= akāsi). Abhinihāro = patthanā.

l. 2. Sivindo]—*i.e.*, Sivirājā Vessantaro. Vide *Vessantarajātakaṃ* for the sacrifice of Madī. *Maddiṃ* for *Madiṃ* is used *metri causa*.

(27) l. 3. Jâtisu.] For *jâtîsu* metri causa.
Kiñcipekaṁ = kiñci + api + ekaṁ.

l. 4. No agamâsi tassa.] The commentator remarks:—"Tâsu ekampi jâtiṁ tassa mahâpurisassa kiñci appamattakampi niratthakaṁ hutvâ na agamâsi. Pâramitâpûraṇavasena va gato."

(30) l. 2. Attana.] For *attânaṁ* metri causa. The line is of thirteen syllables in the Rucirâ metre. The first and third lines are *upavajirâ*, the fourth *indavajirâ*.

(44) l. 2. Varalakkhaṇâni.] This refers to the 32 signs of a great man, the 80 minor characteristics (*anubyanjanâni*), and the 108 footmarks (*mahâmaṅgalalakkhaṇâni*).

(45) l. 2. Avhâyitaṁ.] The *Ṭîkâ* makes this equivalent to *avhâyantaṁ* and *pakkosantaṁ*, "calling," "summoning," and is taken as qualifying *pabbajituṁ*. "Ehi maṁ viya pabbajâhî ti avhâyantaṁ pakkosantaṁ viya pabbajâyarûpaṁ disvâ ti attho." The Burmese *Nissaya* takes *avhâyitaṁ* as qualifying *mataṁ* in the sense of "wrapped in a shroud." The readings *âvhâyitaṁ* and *avhayikaṁ* are also met.

(46) l. 1. Vaḍḍhite = bhogayasissariyâdîhi vaḍḍhite.

(47) l. 2. Purakkhito.] This as well as the reading *purekkhito* occurs. For *pâritthîhi* two MSS. read *varitthîhi*, "by excellent women."

Namo tassa.] This palindromic invocation, which reads forwards and backwards the same, was furnished, the commentator says, by Buddharakkhita for the Mâgadhî people, that by its repetition they may exercise their devotion to Buddha in contemplation of his various attributes of perfection.

(49) l. 1. Mada.] *Mada* is of four kinds—*yobbana*, *ârogya*, *jîvita*, and *râga*.

l. 2. Rata.] "Pleasure," as in Sanskrit. The reading occurs only in one MS., but I have retained it as being in keeping with the rhyme. The reading *rati* occurs in the other MSS.

(50) l. 1. Paditta.] "Burning," "blazing," from $\sqrt{}$dip with *pa*.

l. 2. Mahesî.] According to the commentator *Mahesî* = "one who seeks the road to Nirvâṇa." Mahesî = "one who seeks her husband's great welfare."

l. 4. Tanosi no.] "Did not extend;" hence "did not make manifest."

(51) l. 1. Ummâra.] "Threshold," and metaphorically = "uttarito Mâro" and "uppâṭito Mâro."

l. 4. Mativeti = me + ativa + eti.
Anaṅga = "Kâmarâga," "Anaṅgadevatâ" ("God of Love").

(52) l. 2. Samacintayittha.] "Reflected well."

(53) l. 1. Sâdhya = sâdhitabba.

(54) l. 1. Âdittaṁ.] "Burnt by the eleven fires of *Kilesa*."
Uyyâta.] "Maccumukhe gamanasajjitaṁ."
Payâtaṁ.] "Caturoghehi taritaṁ."

(54) l. 1. Ûnaṁ.] "Uno loko atitto tanhâ daso ti vuttattâ unaṁ apûritaṁ." *Unaṁ* for ûnaṁ is frequent in Bur. MSS.

(55) l. 2. Añjanaṁ.] "Black like collyrium;" hence "ignorant." "Añjanaṁ janan ti ativiya kaṇhadhammasammâpannaṁ janaṁ."

(56) l. 1. Apavaggaṁ.] "Nirvâṇa."

l. 2. Tevâhu = Te + eva + âhu.

(58) l. 2. Tameva.] Taṁ = taṁ sattasantânaṁ.

(59) l. 2. Sayambhu.] The glossarial rendering of this word is "*sayameva jânanto.*"

l. 4. Sutaṁ sutantaṁ.] "That renowned son" (sutaṁ sutaṁ taṁ). Instead of *sutaṁ*, "renowned," one of my copies has sukaṁ, "own."

(60) l. 1. Dibbacakkaṁ.] This refers to the *Dibbacakkaratana* of a *Cakkavatti* monarch, of which Siddhattha would be the possessor, according to the prediction of the Brahmans, if he did not forsake the world.

l. 2. Khuracakkaṁ.] "Taṁ dibbacakkaṁ antavaṭṭato dukkhato âsaṁ ukkhipituṁ adânâuato khuracakkamâlaṁ viya mama upaṭṭhâti."

Sasârajjaṁ.] This word is explained by *sabhayakaraṁ*. A MS. reads *saṁsârajjaṁ*.

(61) l. 1. Satthiri.] The following note is from *Gulatthadîpanî*:—"Vijjamânasirisattalâ ratanehi samujjalantaṁ vasatipâsâdaṁ mahâhalâhalavisaṁ sirisapâgâraṁ yasmâ mâlâdâmaṁ viya sobhamâno pi sirisapo daṭṭhaluṭṭhakâle halâhalavisoyeva tathâ evarûpopi pâsâdo maṁ palobhetvâ taṇhaṁ vaḍḍhetvâ saṁsâre osîdâpanato ayameva halâhalaviso." By taking *vasati* for "palace," instead of as the present participle feminine of $\sqrt{}$vas, "to live," the translation undergoes some alteration.

l. 2. Sirisapâgâraṁ = sarisapa + âgâraṁ. Bur. MSS. have either *sirisapa* (*Sk.* sarisṛipa) or *sarisapa*, but not *siriṁsapa*. Two of my MSS. have *âkâraṁ* for *âgâraṁ*.

l. 3. Vatimâ = vati + imâ.

l. 4. Samañjasa.] "Good," "pure." The reading *samanjusa* also occurs.

(62) l. 2. Tittivasânanamatthi = titti + avasânaṁ + atthi.

l. 4. Mattebha = matta + ibha, "elephant."

(63) l. 1. Panuṇṇa.] This, and not *panunna*, is the reading in my MSS.

l. 2. Bâṇâni.] This is explained by *Pañca kâmaguṇikaṁ râgaṁ*, and *nirodha*, at the end of the line, by *nirujjha*.

l. 3. Câpâdagato = ca + apâdagato.

(64) l. 4. Tahiṁ.] The first *tahiṁ* = *ta* + *ahiṁ*; the second signifies "there," "somewhere."

(67) l. 3. Pitarañjanaggaṁ = pitaraṁ + jana + aggaṁ.

(70) l. 1. Saroje = padume, "what is produced in a pond."

(70) l. 1. Aḷipāḷi.] The usual spelling in Bur. MSS. is *oli*, "a bee," and *pāḷi*, "a row."

l. 2. Pañjarañjasā = "sīhapañjaramaggena."

l. 4. Lajjā.] Archaic form for *lijjāya*.

Saṁkujanti.] The same as *saṁkucanti*.

(72) l. 3. Atiricca.] "Exceeding," from √rich, "to pass."

l. 4. Vaṇitā.] The same as *vanitā*.

(73) l. 1. Sañcodita.] "Urging," "inciting."

l. 2. Aṅgaja.] "Itthiliṅga."

Akhalā.] "Those not base;" "*adujjanārasasatiyo*," "*adujjanarasaṅgaṇiyo*."

l. 3. Vaṅgaja = va + aṅgaja. Phassadā = methunasamphassadāyikā.

l. 4. Varaṅgadāgadā = *vara* + aṅga + dā + agadā, "as medicine." A free translation of the last two lines of stanza 72 is all that could be attempted.

(75) l. 1. Hasula.] "Charming," "attractive." (Sk. *harshaṇa* and *harshula* from √hṛish.)

Sumajjhā.] "Slender-waisted," "having fine waists." (*Sk.* sumadhya.)

(76) l. 2. Kathāvakāsā = kathā + avakāsā.

(77) l. 1. Pādepāde = pāde + apāde.

l. 3. Sambhamanti.] "Whirl" (*Sk.* sam + √bhram).

(78) l. 1. Opacitena = upacitena, "accumulated."

(81) l. 1. Vidhippakāsā.] "Bringing or indicating greatness;" "*puññappabhāvadīpakā*."

Nidhiyo catasso.] The four jars that come into existence at a Bodhisat's birth.

l. 3. Sudhāsā.] From *Sudhā* and *āso*, "Feeders on ambrosia." "Suddhābbhojanaṁ bhuñjanakā devā ye cakkavāḷaparicchinne loke atthi te sabbe cakkavattibhūtassa anuvattakā honti." —*Gūḷatthadīpanī.*

(82) l. 3. Vilāsinihi.] Ins. fem. pl. of *vilāsī*, "charming."

(83) l. 3. Suvijjita.] This I take as equivalent to suvījita, "well fanned." *Suvijjitaṅgo* may, however, simply mean "possessed of an excellent body;" in which case the translation will need slight modification.

(85) l. 4. Himabindusamāni.] "Like drops of dew," *i.e.*, "inconsequential."

(86) l. 4. Mahita.] Some texts read *namito*.

Purisassarehi = purisa + issarehi. One MS. has *asurissarehi*.

(87) l. 2. Anaṅga.] The God of Love, Manobhū, typifying *Kāmarāga*.

Dhaja.] With the *makara* displayed on it.

(88) l. 2. Kusa.] Kusarājā loved Pabhāvatī, the daughter of the Madda king. Although he was the most exalted king of Jambudīpā, he yet worked as a slave in her house, conveying the food-trays on a rice-pole, but he got no opportunity of seeing

her. Sakka, admiring his devotion, eventually intervened, and so Kusa obtained Pabhâvati. *Vide* "Kusajâtakaṁ."

(89) l. 2. Varaṁ.] Pres. Part. of *varuti*, "desires," "solicits," "woos."

Anitthigandho.] *Vide* "Anitthigandhajâtakaṁ." This Prince of Benares was so called because he had an inveterate aversion to women from the time of his birth. When he attained the age of sixteen a dancing-girl enticed him, and he lived with her. After that he wished to monopolise the love of women, and went about slaughtering men. Anitthigandha and the dancing-girl were expelled by the king, and had to live in the forest.

l. 3. Riñcâpi = *riñci* + *api*. *Riñci* is the Aor. of the √ric, "to abandon" (2nd Conj.).

(90) l. 1. Harittaco.] "The hermit with the golden-coloured skin." He was the confidential adviser of the King of Benares. On one occasion, when the latter went to suppress a rebellion, Haritaca came into the palace, and happening to see his queen, Paduma, nude, forgot his vow of chastity. *Harittaco* is used for *Haritaco* on account of the versification.

(91) l. 2. Varitthiṁ.] Sivali, Madi, and others.

l. 3. Aṇuṁ kaliṁ.] "A small stake." *Kali* is used here in the sense of "something subject to calculation."

l. 4. Tunnakâro.] "A tailor." "Tunnakâro sâṭakam pattharitvâ chiddamera oloketi evaṁ bhagavâ aṇuṁ kaliṁ vaṇṇayi." Some MSS. read *tuṇṇakâro*.

(92) l. 1. Tathâ ti]—*i.e.*, with regard to Buddha as Kusa, Anitthigandha, &c.

l. 4. Ñâṇa = Âdinavânupassanâñâṇa.

Antaraṁ.] "Occasion," "opportunity;" *Kâraṇaṁ*. The reference is to the *Catubbidhanimittaṁ*.

(93) l. 4. Padaṁ.] Here used in two senses—(1) *means*, (2) *Nirvâṇa*.

(94) l. 4. Tathâgato.] "He who went away thus," *i.e.*, by renouncing the world.

(95) l. 2. Tathâgato.] Anaṅga, who went away defeated.

l. 3. Tathâgato.] Bodhisatto.

l. 4. Diavânañâṇa = diavâna + añâṇa.

(96) l. 2. Himâropita = hi + m + âropita.

Dâha.] The burning of the *Kilesas*.

l. 3. Tadâha = tadâ + âha. This refers to the occasion when Mâra, discomfited in his efforts to find fault with the Bodhisat, sat on the high-road contemplating the virtues of the Blessed One and drawing a line on the ground for each one of them. When his daughters, Taṇhâ, Arati, and Ragâ, declared that they would entice the Bodhisat, Mâra gave utterance to the well-known words—"Arahaṁ sugato loke," &c.

l. 4. Mâropi = mâ + âropi.

Tadâ.] When the daughters of Mâra used their enticements.

Hasantiṁ.] Acc. of hasanti, f., "laughing."

(97) In this stanza:—

Sa = his; own; with.

kâma = sensual pleasure; desire.

dâtâ = giving; a giver.

adâtâ = not giving; destroying.

[datâvi = giving.]

vinaya = restraint; instruction; the Scriptures; law; various ways; diverse means.

[Naya = way; means.]

Mana = mind; thought; intention; wish.

anta = end; inferior; low; consummation; Nirvâṇa.

ananta = infinitude; perfect knowledge (*sabbaññutaññâṇa*); the end of *Kilesas*.

gû = gato.

manantaṁ = antaṁ + manaṁ.

vinayamanantagû = vinaya + m + anantagû.

N.B.—Vinaya, "various ways," is explained by the *Sattatiṁsa bodhipakkhiyâ dhammâ* in relation to the attainment of Nirvâṇa, and by *arahattaphala* and *vimuttiñâṇa* with regard to the attainment of perfect knowledge. The *Ṭîkâ*, in answer to the question, What does Buddha give to man in gratification of his wishes? (*sakâma* in the fourth *pâda*), replies, "Tiṁsatchasatanavayojanasata parimâṇesu anto majjhimamahâmaṇḍalesu cârikaṁ caranto dhammabheriṁ paharanto dhammasaṅkhaṁ dhamanto dhammadhajaṁ ussâpento sîhanâdaṁ nadanto dhammacakkaṁ pavattento uttamaṁ saccarasapânaṁ pâyento bodhaneyyakamalâkâraṁ vibhodento kesañci saraṇagamanaṁ deti; kesañci pañcasîlaṁ pabbajjaṁ upasampadaṁ dadanto kesañci rûpârûpajjhânaṁ kesañci vipassanâmaggaphalanibbânaṁ dadanto sakalaloke sâsanaṁ pattharati."

(98) The following is an analysis of this *abyapetadutiyantayamaka* stanza:—

FIRST PÂDA.—Rave = pharusavacane.

Avero = verarahita, "free from enmity," referring to *jino*. Rave + avero = raveravero, *r* being a euphonic insertion.

Abhimâra = the great Mâra; Vasavatti-Mâra.

Bherave = in harshness; in terror.

SECOND PÂDA.—Ravera = raveraṁ = ravi + iraṁ, "the quaking of the sun." *Iraṁ* is the present participle of *irati*, "moves," "shakes."

Vere = in an enemy; in regard to an enemy (such as Râhu).

Vereriva = vere + r + iva.

Bherave = terrified (with sufferings in hell, &c.).

Rave (acc. pl.) = the crying ones (in hell, &c., who wish to be rescued from transmigration), *i.e.*, gods and men. *Rave* is governed by *avedesi* in the fourth *pâda*.

THIRD PÂDA.—Rave rave = (bhagavato) vuttavuttapâvacane.
Sûdita = su + udita = "well spoken."
gârave = "respectful."
Rave (loc.) = in supplication; in crying.

FOURTH PÂDA.—Raveravedesi = rave + r + avedesi. *Rave*, appositional acc. "the crying ones," *i.e.*, "gods and men;" *avedesi* = *bodhesi* = *jânâpesi*.
Jinorave = Jino + orave, "not noisy," "not boisterous," hence "gentle," "respectful."
Rave (acc.) = "words;" "utterances," governed by *avedesi*.

(99) l. 1. Visesaṁ saṁsevi = vibhaji, "distinguished himself," "followed a distinguished course of action," *i.e.*, by being Bodhisat and Buddha and ultimately attaining Nirvâṇa, and providing a religious dispensation for five thousand years.
Na na.] The two negatives neutralise each other.

N.B.—This and the following are *paṭilomayamaka* or palindromic stanzas, *i.e.*, stanzas in which the words are the same if read forwards or backwards.

(100) l. 1. Râjarâja.] Buddha, "the King of Kings."
Yasopeta = yaso + upeta.
l. 2. Yâma.] Here used for *yâmi*, with a future signification.
Cirasaṁsevitapeso = ciraṁ saṁseviṁ tapo eso. Here *eso* = eso ahaṁ, the author of *Jinâlaṅkâra*.
Yajarâjarâ = yaṁ ajaraṁ ajarâ (abl.). Take *yâva* as understood with *ajarâ*, "until I attain Nirvâṇa."

N.B.—According to the commentator *saṁsevi* and *tapa* are taken as *saṁseviṁ* and *tapaṁ*, adjectives qualifying taṁ = bhagavantaṁ, and *ajaraṁ* is differently employed. "Mayâ jinâlaṅkâraṁ karontena yaṁ râjarâjayasopetaṁ visesaṁ racitaṁ tena puññena yâvâhaṁ nibbânaṁ pâpuṇâmi tâva ajaraṁ navaṁ navaṁ katvâ taṁ ciraṁ saṁsevitapaṁ bhagavantaṁ saraṇaṁ gacchâmi." On *yaṁ* the following note is given:—"Yaṁ saddo paṭhamapadena sambandhaṁ gacchati."

(101) l. 1. Âkaṅkhakkhâkaṅkhaṅga = Âkaṅkha + akkha, "organ of sense" + akaṅkha + aṅga. Here *âkaṅkha* refers to *paṭibandhaanâvaraṇañâṇaṁ*. Akaṅkhaṅga = kaṅkhavicchedakalakkhaṇabyañjanasamannâgatasarîra.
Gaṅgâkhâgahaka = gaṅgâ, "river" + kha ("destroying") + agahaka, "not accepting." "Pabandhuppattiyâ kaṅkhâ yâ gaṅgâ tassâ abhâvagâhaka."
l. 2. Kaṅkhâgha = kaṅkhâvinâsaka.
Hâ hâ, &c.] "Alas! alas! where can there be doubt in me," *i.e.*, "I should without doubt accept the teachings of Buddha." The alternative rendering of the line is, "Alas! alas! where can there be doubt in thee."

(102) l. 1. Apagabbho.] (1) Apagatagabbho, punabbhavarahito; (2) na pagabbho, kâyapâgabbhiyâdirahito.

l. 2. Maggamukhaṁ mokhaṁ = arahattamaggadvârena pavisitabbaṁ nibbânaṁ. One MS. reads *aggamukhaṁ*.

Mohamûbhakkhanaṁ = mohavaḍḍhanakaṁ kathaṁ.

(103) l. 2. Bhavâsaṅgâ = bhava + asaṅgâ (abl.). Asaṅgâ = anâlayâ.

(105) l. 1. Nonânino = no, "our" + ananino, dat. of anâni from anana, "breathing," "living." Anâni, "the living or breathing one," *i.e.*, Buddha, supposed to be the living one who imparts to creatures the breath of Nirvâṇa. The comment has "Ananti anâ pajâ assâsapassâsamattaṁ karonti ti attho; te anena yatiṁ nibbânaṁ pâpeti ti anâni, bhagavâ."

Nanûnâni = nanu, "surely" + unâni, "deficiencies."

Nanenâni = na + anenâni or na + a + enâni, pl. of enaṁ, "sin," "fault."

Nanânino = na + anânino as before.

l. 2. Nunnânenâni = nunnâni, "removed" + enâni, "sins," "faults."

Nânanaṁ = na + ânanaṁ, "face," "mouth."

Nânanena = na + ânanena.

(106) l. 1. Sâri.] "Remembrancer" by means of religious teaching.

Rasasâra.] Explained by the 9 *Lokuttaradhammas*.

l. 2. Sâri.] "Completing," "filling up," from $\sqrt{sṛ}$.

Rasasârarase.] An allusion to Arhatship or Nirvâṇa.

(107) l. 2. Vedadinena.] "By knowledge being deficient," "through deficiency of knowledge." The occasion referred to is when Buddha went to preach the "Abhidhamma" to the devas, and Sakka considered his throne far too big for him.

Vedena vedi, &c.] The sentence is elliptical. "By his knowledge he knew his own weakness; by the wisdom of Buddha the thoughts of Sakka were discovered." Vedino = "of the Buddha." The *Ṭîkâ* has the following note:—"Paññavato bhagavato paññânubhâvena tassajjhâsayaṁ ñatvâ sakalaṁ âsanaṁ (paṇḍukambalasilâ) paṭicchâdetvâ nisinnabhâvena paṭiladdhasaṁvego sakko attano paññâya dubbalaṁ jâni."

(108) l. 1. Devâsane.] The *paṇḍukambalasilâ* on which Buddha took his seat on the occasion referred to in the previous stanza.

(109) l. 1. Dasanâva = dasana, "tooth" + ava, "speech," "lip." Dasanâvagato, "coming from the teeth and lips," *i.e.*, "a word that is uttered."

Sañño.] Here a synonym for *nâmo*, "having a name," and referring to Buddha. The stanza is a "paheli" or enigmatical stanza, and words are therefore employed which depart from ordinary usage.

Tamado = tama + ado, "destroying," "removing."

l. 2. Aṭṭhamâpuṇṇasaṅkappo = aṭṭhama + âpuṇṇasaṅkappo, *i.e.*, Buddha, who is replete with the thoughts of the eight *ariyapuggalas*, or who has accomplished his aim by the attainment of Arhatship.

Pátvanaññamanaññiva' = pátu + anaññaṁ + anaññi + iva. Pátu = rakkhatu; anaññaṁ, "not another," *i.e.*, "myself;" anaññi, "not another," *i.e.*, "himself."

(110) l. 3. Márabalena.] The *Tíká* has *khandhakilesábhisaṅkháramaccudevaputtasaṅkhátamárabalena.*

(114) l. 2. Majjhimáya = majjhimáya paṭipadáya, "by the mediocre path of Arhatship"—*mediocre* as not requiring such severe efforts as were put forth at the time of previous great penances and sacrifices.

l. 4. Dhammaṁ.] The exercise of *samádhi*.

(115) l. 1. Tisetachatte.] (1) Mánussikachattaṁ, (2) Devachattaṁ, (3) Arahattachattaṁ.

(118) l. 1. Náráyanabalo.] Náráyana's strength is represented as being equal to 10,000 *koṭis* of elephants.

(120) l. 2. Manussakalalo.] "Esa manussitthiyá kucchismiṁ sukkasoṇitasaṅkháte kalale puttmaṁse játakimi viya játo."

(128) l. 1. Saso.] *Vide* "Sasajátakaṁ."

(132) l. 1. Anupalitto.] "Lokenapi lokesu kenápi sattena vá saṅkhárena vá anupalitto analliño hutvá játo."

(133) l. 1. Saváhanaṁ.] "Girimekhalahatthisaṁhitaṁ."

(135) l. 1. Icchanto.] This stanza is to show Buddha's miraculous power (*iddhibalaṁ*). All the MSS. have *cháḷayi*.

(138) l. 2. Sakkhi.] This reference is to the occasion when, seated on the Bodhi throne, Siddhattha asked Mára for a witness to his alms, and his followers with one voice cried, "I am witness, I am witness, I am witness!" Mára then asked the Bodhisat for a witness to his bestowal of alms. The Bodhisat appealed to the earth as his witness in relation to his sacrifice of his wife Madi in his birth as Vessantara.

(140) l. 1. Gajjanto asani.] One MS. reads *gajjantá asani.*

l. 2. Tasmiṁ majjhe.] "Tasmiṁ pathavíákásánaṁ abbhantare gato."

(141) l. 1. Vikiriyyatha.] Used for *vikiriyatha metri causa* = vikiriyaṁ pápuṇittha.

l. 2. Ajáyittha.] The reading *ajáyatha* also occurs.

(142) l. 1. Purato, &c.] This stanza refers to the time of day when the victory over Mára was achieved. "Vasavattimáraṁ parájetvá nisinne mahásamudde nimujjamánaṁ suvaṇṇacakkaṁ viya sahassaraṁsi súriyo pacchimadisáyaṁ apagacchati atthaṅgameti; cakkaváḷagabbhaṁ khíraságare nipujjápayamano viya pabhásamudayaṁ vissajjento anilapathe ullaṅghiyamáno rajatacakkaṁ viya pácinadisáyaṁ ambare upagacchati."—*Guḷatthadípaní.* The *Tíká* has:—"Evaṁ Vasavattimáraṁ parájitvá nisinnasakaladasasahassacakkaváḷavásino bhútádayo devatá saddamanussáhesuṁ—'Etha márisá

Siddhatthassa 'mārassa parājayo jayamaṅgalañca Buddhamaṅgalañca ekato karissāmā' ti ekappahārena va samosarimsu; tasmiṁ khaṇe paññāsayojanappamāṇaṁ raṁsisahassupasobhitaṁ suriyamaṇḍalaṁ nemiyaṁ gahetvā mahāsamudde nimujjāpayamānaṁ suvaṇṇaṁ cakkaṁ viya atthaṁ gacchantaṁ ṭhitaṁ; ekūnapaññāsayojanappamāṇaṁ pabhāsamudayavisajjantaṁ caṇḍamaṇḍalaṁ cakkavāḷagabbhaṁ khīrasāgare nimujjāpayamānaṁ nemiyaṁ gahetvā anilapathe ullaṅghiyamānaṁ rajatacakkaṁ viya pācinadisato uggacchantaṁ ṭhitaṁ"

(146) l. 1. Abhidhāvati.] "Runs towards the *Bodhimaṇḍala*."

(157) l. 1. Yathākammupage = "Sakasakakammānurūpena uppajjante satte."

(158) l. 1. Ñāṇantaṁ = ñāṇaṁ + taṁ.

l. 2. Tenasesā = tena + asesā (abl.).

Solasadhā]—*i.e.*, the 5 doubts of the past, 5 of the future, and 6 of the present. "Yā pi pubbantaṁ ārabbha ahosi nu kho ahaṁ atītamaddhānaṁ, na nu kho, kinnu kho, kathaṁ nu kho, kiṁ hutvā kiṁ ahosi nu kho ahaṁ atītamaddhānanti pañcavidhā vicikicchā vuttā; yā pi aparantaṁ ārabbha bhavissāmi nu kho ahaṁ anāgatamaddhānaṁ, na nu kho, kinnu kho, kathaṁ nu kho, kiṁ hutvā kiṁ bhavissāmi nu kho ahaṁ anāgatamaddhānanan ti pañcavidhā vicikicchā vuttā; yā pi paccuppannamaddhānaṁ ārabbha etarahi vā paccuppannaṁ ahaṁ nu khosmiṁ, na nu khosmiṁ, kinnu khosmiṁ, kathaṁ nu khosmiṁ, ayaṁ nu kho satto kuto, so kuhiṁ gāmi bhavissati ti chabbidhā vicikicchā vuttā."

(166) l. 1. Paccayaṁ.] Two of my copies read *dānādiratayaṁ*.

Pure.] "Paṭhamaṁ Dīpaṅkarapādamūlato."

(170) l. 2. Udānudirayī.] The reference is to the well-known verses commencing "Anekajātisaṁsāraṁ." *Dhammapada*, vv. 153-154.

l. 3. Māre]—*i.e.*, *the five Māras*.

(171) l. 3. Mahāsahassaṁ.] The reading *mahāsahassiṁ* also occurs.

(172) l. 1. Lokāloke = loka + āloke.

l. 3. Suddhaṁ buddhaṁ.] MSS. read *buddhaṁ suddhaṁ* also.

(173) l. 1. Bhajitaṁ.] This *Byāpetādyantayamaka* stanza and the stanza previous are omitted in two of my MSS.

l. 4. Namitam, &c.] One MS. reads for the last line:—

Namāmi muniṁ satataṁ niyataṁ.

This is evidently put in to make the stanza syntactically independent of the previous one.

(174) l. 2. Vatamiti = vata + m + iti.

l. 4. Brahmenāyācito = Brahmena + āyācito. The reading *brahmenā yācito* is also found.

Dhammacakkaṁ.] Buddha's first sermon was the well-known *Dhammacakkapavattanasuttaṁ*. *Dhammacakkaṁ vattayi* (or *pavattayi*) signifies "Established the Domain of Law," and thence "Set forth the supreme truths of religion." *Cakka*, the symbol of supreme dominion, is taken as a transferred epithet for dominion itself. *Vattayi*, in this connection, is found paraphrased by *desesi*.

(176) l. 2. Vasi.] "Versed," "accomplished."

l. 4. Anukampimaṁ = anukampā (abl. of *anukampo*, "pity") + imaṁ.

(177) l. 2. Sanarāmarānaṁ = sa + nara + amarānaṁ. The reading *sanaramarānaṁ* is also found.

l. 3. Nānānayehibhisamesi = nānānayehi + abhisamesi. The vowel is lengthened on account of the metre.

Abhisamesi.] *Gulatthadīpanī* has:—"Abhisamayaṁ lokuttaramaggaphalādhigamaṁ pāpesi," taking the meaning from √i, "to go," but *abhisameti* also technically signifies "appeases the suffering of transmigration."

l. 4. Jhāto.] "Known," "reputed."

(178) l. 2. Diṭṭhā pattā ñātā saccāni.] "Catusaccaṁ cakkhunā rūpaṁ viya diṭṭhā hatthatalappattaṁ viya pattā ñāṇena ñātā."

l. 4. Thomesuṁ.] The praises bestowed upon Buddha are as follows:—

"Tuvaṁ Buddho tuvaṁ satthā
tuvaṁ Mārābhibhumuni
tuvaṁ anusaye chetvā
tiṇṇo tāresidaṁ pajaṁ."

"Upadhi te samatikkantā
Āsavā te padālitā
Sīhosi anupādāno
pahīnabhayabheravo."

"Tuvaṁ satthā ca ketu ca
dhajo yuvo anuttaro
parāyano patiṭṭhā ca
dīpo dvipaduttamo."

(180) l. 1. Rutā = *kathitā*. The reading *gaṇchi rutā* is also found.

l. 3. Gahaṇā.] This is explained in the *Ṭīkā* by *anekesaṁ mukhena nirantaraṁ kathitā*.

(181) l. 3. Navavidhesu padesu.] As in the well-known formula:—"Itipi so bhagavā arahaṁ sammāsambuddho vijjācaraṇasampanno sugato lokavidū anuttaro purisadammasārathi satthā devamanussānaṁ buddho bhagavā."

(182) l. 4. Sugato.] This epithet is explained by "sundaraṭṭhānaṁ gato," i.e., "He who has gone to Nirvāṇa." *Sundaraṭṭhānaṁ* is also explained by *bodhipallaṅkaṭṭhānaṁ*.

(184) l. 3. Yadatthi ñeyyaṁ = yaṁ ñeyyaṁ atthi. The five *ñeyyadhammas or intuitive principles of knowledge* are *saṅkhāra, vikāra, lakkhaṇa, nibbāna*, and *viññatti*.

(185) l. 3. Payuta.] This word should be construed with *anantakkhaṁ*. The gloss in the *Ṭīkanissaya* reads *passata*, "of those who can see." The reading *payutta* also occurs.

l. 4. Tadihu] = *Tad*, refers to *Sugatabodhi*.

(188) l. 4. Netaṁ = ne + etaṁ. Stanza 187 is not found in one of my palm-leaf MSS.

(189) l. 1. Jātovarakamhi = jāta + ovarakamhi.

(195) l. 1. Salala.] Also salaḷa.

(196) l. 1. Makulā.] Also vakulā, vakkulā, bakulā.

(201) l. 2. Kūjanti.] Also kuñcanti, "they warble."

(202) l. 1. Niccharāṇaṁ.] Also nijjarāṇaṁ.

(204) l. 2. Kariyati.] Also kariyyati.

(206) l. 2. Kekayā.] Used *metri causa* for Kekāyā. Two of my MSS. read *kekaṁ*.

(207) l. 2. Vijambhitena.] Ins. of vijambhitaṁ, "sport."

Gītiyā.] Childers gives *gītikā*, the diminutive of *gīti* (f.). "a song."

(208) l. 2. Dhūpiyā.] This I take to be the *ins.* of a fem. *dhūpi*, "perfume."

(209) l. 1. Susamphulla.] This word, which is the same as in Sanskrit, is equal to *susamphullita*.

(210) l. 2. Sāmuddikaṁ.] "Marine," "appertaining to the sea."

(211) l. 2. Masāragallaṁ.] The form *masārakallaṁ* is mostly met with in Burmese MSS.

(215) l. 2. Kapiṭṭhā.] "Wood apples," "elephant apples." The word *kapiṭṭha* literally signifies "a monkey station," *i.e.*, the tree *Feronia Elephantum*. The form *kapittha* appears in one of my MSS. Childers has *kaviṭṭha* as well.

Coca.] A generic term for the palm-fruit.

(216) l. 1. Ojaṁ.] "Essence." The gender of the word, as in Sanskrit, is neuter.

(218) l. 2. Carimakaṁ.] "Last," "latest."

(220) l. 1. Āvenikaṁ.] The eighteen *Āveṇikas* are the same as the eighteen *Buddhadhammas* enumerated by Hardy in his "Manual of Buddhism," p. 381. Also *vide* Burnouf's "Lotus," p. 648.

(221) l. 1. Āsayānusayañāṇaṁ.] "The knowledge which understands the thoughts and intentions of others."

Paroparaṁ.] This indeclinable is equivalent to the adverbial ablative *paramparā*, and is a modification of the Vedic *parovaraṁ*.

(222) l. 1. Mahākaruṇa, &c.] This line is also given as follows:—
"Mahākaruṇāsamāpattiñāṇaṁ anāvaraṇamiti."

l. 2. Asādhāraṇānete = asādhāraṇāni + ete.

(225) l. 1. Rammaṁ.] One text reads *varaṁ*.

(226) l. 2. Orohaṇakaṁ.] Also *orohanakaṁ*.

(230) l. 1. Paṇidhānamhi.] Used as equivalent to *paṇidhānato*.

l. 2. Parinibbāyināsavo = parinibbāyi + anāsavo.

(231) l. 2. Nibbáyittha.] The reading *nibbáyoti* occurs in two of my texts.

(232) l. 1. Dhammo]—*i.e.*, the *Suttapitaka* along with the *Abhidhamma-pitaka.* The word often occurs in this sense, unless it be assumed that the *Abhidhamma* was added to Buddha's word as an after compilation by his disciples.

(237) l. 1. Paramparabhatánaṁ.] Instead of *ábhatánaṁ,* some MSS. read *ágatánaṁ.*

(239) l. 2. Lañchanakaṁ.] All the MSS. have *lañcanakaṁ.* This error arises from the fact that the Burmese phonetic system does not admit of any palatal aspirate.

(242) l. 4. Pemaniyo.] The reading *paṇḍito* also is met with, which the metre does not justify.

(243) ll. 3–4. Vajirúpamátipaññá = vajirúpamá + atipaññá.

(244) l. 4. Accapalo.] The readings *apacalo* and *appacalo* also occur.

(245) l. 1. Bhaveyyahaṁ = bhaveyyaṁ + ahaṁ.
l. 2. Bhogo, &c.] Two MSS. read for the second line " bhogo ca dinnehi vibhavo-m-anūno."

(248) l. 1. Anúpalitto.] This is used for *anupalitto* for the sake of the metre, and is equivalent to the form *anuppallito,* which one of my MSS. has.

(249) l. 2. Kareyyakhantiṁ = kareyyaṁ + khantiṁ.

(250) l. 1. Pañca]—*i.e., property, wife, children, dominion,* and *life.*

APPENDIX

(A.) METRES OF THE *JINÂLAṄKÂRA*.

I. Octosyllabic Dissimilar Quarter-Verses.

(a) *Vatta.*

Free.	Trisyllabic.	Trisyllabic.	Free.
x	*y*	*z*	*x*
x	*y*	◡ — ◡	*x*
x	*y*	*z*	*x*
x	*y*	◡ — ◡	*x*

(b) *Pathyâvatta.*

x	*y*	◡ — —	*x*
x	*y*	◡ — ◡	*x*
x	*y*	◡ — —	*x*
x	*y*	◡ — ◡	*x*

N.B.—*x* = ◡ or — but sometimes dissyllabic; *y* = any trisyllabic foot except ◡ ◡ — or ◡ ◡ ◡; *z* = any trisyllabic foot.

The following stanzas have an additional syllable in the free member:—105 (4th Pâda), 117 (4th P.), 121 (2nd P.), 139 (1st P.), 140 (1st and 4th P.), 142 (2nd P.), 145 (1st P.), 149 (3rd P.), 153 (2nd P.), 155 (4th P.), 160 (1st P.), 169 (3rd P.), 202 (3rd P.), 220 (3rd and 4th P.), 222 (1st. P.), 224 (1st P.), 228 (1st P.), 231 (3rd P.).

The following furnish examples of the odd pâdas running into the even pâdas:—Stanzas 141, 152, 228, 229.

The free syllable is wanting in stanzas 164 and 241, the former having seven syllables in the fourth pâda and the latter seven in the second pâda.

Irregularities.

Stanza 141 has ⏑ ⏑ – in the 2nd foot of the 2nd pâda, 162 has ⏑ – –, 169 has – – ⏑, 218 has ⏑ ⏑ ⏑ in the second foot of the 4th pâda, 220 has – – ⏑ in the 2nd foot of the 2nd pâda. The inflectional vowel î is shortened for the sake of the metre, as *jâtisu* for *jâtîsu* (v. 161), *vâpisu* for *vâpîsu* (v. 191), *hatthinaṁ* for *hatthînaṁ* (v. 207), &c.

II. Octosyllabic Similar Quarter-Verses.

Vijjummâlâ.

– – | – – | – – | – –

Examples.—Stanzas 172, 178, 188.

III. Stanzas of 11 Syllables.

(a) *Indavajirâ.*

– – ⏑ | – – ⏑ | ⏑ – ⏑ | – ⏓

Examples.—Stanzas 4, 54, 56, 177, 182.

(b) *Upavajirâ.*

⏑ – ⏑ | – – ⏑ | ⏑ – ⏑ | – ⏓

Examples.—Stanzas 94, 96, 112, 183.

(c) *Dodhaka.*

– ⏑ ⏑ | – ⏑ ⏑ | – ⏑ ⏑ | – –

Example.—Stanza 48.

Upajâti Stanzas.

Upajâti stanzas, made up of (a) and (b), present a large variety. *Examples.*—6, 7, 12, 14, 27, 28, 30, 39, 40, 51, 52, 57, 58, 59, 70, 74, 75, 83, 84, 111, 114, 171, 187, 243, 244, 245.

IV. Stanzas of 12 Syllables.

(a) *Vaṁsaṭṭha.*

⏑ – ⏑ | – – ⏑ | ⏑ – ⏑ | – ⏑ –

Examples.—Stanzas 97, 98.

It also forms Upajâti stanzas in combination with Indavajirâ or Upavajirâ, or both. *Examples.*—8 (1st Pâda), 9 (1st and 2nd P.), 13 (1st and 2nd P.), 16 (4th P.), 37 (1st P.), 38 (1st and 3rd P.), 50 (3rd and 4th P.), 55 (2nd and 4th P.), 61 (1st, 2nd, and 4th P.), 64 (3rd P.), 80 (2nd P.), 81 (2nd P.), 87 (1st P.), 88 (1st P.), 90 (1st and 2nd P.), 92 (4th P.), 93 (3rd P.), 113 (4th P.), 190 (4th P.), 175 (4th P.).

(b) *Toṭaka.*

⏑ ⏑ — | ⏑ ⏑ — | ⏑ ⏑ — | ⏑ ⏑ —

Examples.—Stanzas 173, 179, 180.

It also appears in stanza 71, but the 1st and 3rd pâdas have a foot deficient.

The following do not occur in all the quarter-verses :—

(i) *Indavaṁsa.*

— — ⏑ | — — ⏑ | — — ⏑ | — — ⏑

Examples.—Stanzas 10 (2nd and 3rd Pâda), 11 (1st P.), 15 (3rd and 4th P.), 17 (4th P.), 18 (4th P.), 19 (2nd P.), 21 (2nd and 4th P.), 36 (1st and 2nd P.), 41 (1st P.), 49 (1st P.), 53 (4th P.), 60 (3rd P.), 73 (1st. P.), 78 (3rd P.), 79 (1st and 2nd P.), 82 (2nd P.), 87 (3rd P.), 88 (3rd P.), 89 (4th P.), 93 (1st P.), 95 (1st and 4th P.), 115 (3rd P.), 190 (2nd P.), 176 (4th P.), 189 (4th P.), 209 (4th P.), 248 (2nd P.). The metre comes in combination with *Indavajirâ*, *Upavajirâ*, and *Vaṁsaṭṭha* quarter-verses.

(ii) *Kamalâ.*

⏑ ⏑ — | ⏑ — — | ⏑ ⏑ — | ⏑ — —

Example.—Stanza 91 (1st Pâda).

V. Stanzas of 14 Syllables.

Vasantatilakâ.

— — ⏑ | — ⏑ ⏑ | ⏑ — ⏑ | ⏑ — ⏑ | — ⏓

Examples.—23, 24, 26, 31, 62, 65, 66, 67, 68, 85, 86, 87, 88, 110, 181. This metre also occurs in the fourth pâdas of stanzas 69 and 76.

VI. Stanza of 15 Syllables.

Malinî.

⏑ ⏑ ⏑ | ⏑ ⏑ ⏑ | — — — | ⏑ — — | ⏑ — —

Example.—Stanza 185, but the 3rd pâda presents some irregularity, the 8th and 9th syllables being ⏑, ⏑ instead of —, —.

VII. Stanza of 17 Syllables.

Mandakkantâ.

— — — | — ⏑ ⏑ | ⏑ ⏑ ⏑ | — — ⏑ | — — ⏑ | — —

Examples.—Stanzas 172, 178, 188.

VIII. Stanza of 19 Syllables.

Saddullavikkiḷitâ.

— — — | ⏑ ⏑ — | ⏑ — ⏑ | ⏑ ⏑ — | — — ⏑ | — — ⏑ | —

Examples.—Stanzas 3 and 186. The cæsura falls after the 13th syllable.

IX. Stanza of 21 Syllables.

Saddharâ.

— — — | — ⏑ — | — ⏑ ⏑ | ⏑ ⏑ ⏑ | ⏑ — — | ⏑ — — | ⏑ — —

Examples.—Stanzas 1, 2, 22, 174. The cæsura falls after the 7th and the 14th syllable.

Irregularities.

Stanza 11 has ⏑ — — in the third foot of the third pâda, stanza 20 — — — in the first foot of the third pâda, stanza 64 has the trisyllabic foot — ⏑ ⏑ in the fourth foot of the fourth pâda, stanza 184 has its first quarter-verse as follows :—

⏑ — ⏑ | ⏑ — ⏑ | ⏑ ⏑ — | ⏑ — ⏑

which forms no recognised metre. Line second of stanza 30 appears doubtful, but I take it to be Rucirâ as follows :—

⏑ — ⏑   — ⏑ ⏑ ⏑ ⏑ — ⏑ — ⏑ —
hitâya   attanamabhiropitakkhaṇe.

The first line of stanza 250 appears defective.

(B.) WORDS AND FORMS NOT IN CHILDERS' DICTIONARY.

STANZA.

2 Natvâna—ger. of √*nam*, "to bow," "to adore."
Suvimha—"very astonishing." [*Sk.* suvismya.]

3 Kamato—"successively," "respectively." [*Sk.* kramaśas.]

4 Âdittaṁ—abs. noun, from *âdi*.

5 Niyamo—"defining," "discernment."

7 Byatita = *vyatîta*, "long past" [vi + ati + ita].

9 Sambhuṇanto—pres. part. of sambhuṇâti, "thinks," "deliberates," from √*bhu*.

11 Asambhi—"without fear," "tranquillising."

12 Anupekkhî—"desiring."

13 Adhicca (*n.*)—"superiority." In the text the word is used with regard to Buddha's inherent superiority of intellect, not dependent on any one else. Hence "underived," "uncaused."

18 Sayi—"lying."

45 Avhâyita—P.P.P. of *avhâyati*, "calls." [*Sk.* âvhâyita.]

47 Purekkhito—a frequently found form in Burmese MSS. for purakkhito.

50 Paditta—P.P.P. of *padippati*, "burns," "blazes."

52 Anaṅga—Kâma, the God of Love; Manobhû.

53 Sâdhya = *sâdhitabba*, from *sâdheti*.

54 Uyâta = uyyâta—P.P.P. of uyyâti.

55 Ûna = una.

59 Sayambhu—"knowing by oneself," "untaught." [Sayaṁ and √bhu, "to know."]

60 Khuracakkaṁ—"a circular razor-like instrument of torture in hell." Cf. "Uracakkaṁ."
Sârajja—"tormenting," "occasioning fear." [Sa + √ard + ya]?

61 Sirîsapa = siriṁsapa.
Samañjasa—"pure," "virtuous."

STANZA.

62 Mattebha (matta + ibha)—"an elephant in rut."

63 Panuṇṇa = panunna.

Bâṇa (*n.*)—"arrow."

67 Saroja—"pond-produced," "lotus."

70 Aḷi—"bee."

Pâḷi—"row."

N.B.—Burmese MSS. give the orthography of both these words correctly. There is nothing in the Burmese phonetic system to allow *l* to pass into *ḷ*.

Saṁkujati—"recoils," "shrinks," from √kuj or √kuc, "to draw back," with *saṁ*.

72 Atiricca (adv. gerund)—"exceedingly," "surpassing," from √ric, "to surpass."

Vaṇitâ = vanitâ.

73 Sañcodita—P.P.P. of sañcodeti = saṁ + codeti.

Aṅgaja = itthiliṅga = aṅgajâta.

75 Hasula and hassula—"charming." [*Sk.* harshula.]

Sumajjha—"slender-waisted." [*Sk.* sumadhya.]

77 Sambhamati—"whirls." [*Sk.* sambhramati.]

78 Opacita = upacita.

80 Pattuṇṇa—"cloth from the kingdom of Pattuṇṇa."

Cîna—"cloth from China;" "China silk"?

81 Sudhâsa—"ambrosia-eating."

82 Vilâsinî (*f.*)—"beautiful," "charming."

83 Vijjita—P.P.P. of vijjati = vijati.

89 Varaṁ—pres. part. of varati, "desires," "solicits."

Riñci—aor. of riñcati, "abandons," from √ric.

91 Kali—score, stake.

Tunnakâro / Tuṇṇakâro }—"a tailor" ("pricker with a needle").

98 Abhimâra—"the great Mâra."

Iraṁ—pres. part. of irati, "moves" (as in *Sk.*).

Avedesi—causal aor. of √vid, "to know."

Orava = avarava—"freedom from noise."

105 Anânino—dat. of anânî, "breathing," adj. from *ananaṁ*.

Enaṁ—"sin."

106 Sârî—"putting in mind," "remembrancer."

STANZA.

108 Pâtu—imperative of pâti, "supports," "maintains." [Vedic √pṛi.]

109 Sañño—"having a name."
Tamado—"destroying gloom," "dispelling darkness."
Ado—"destroying."
Anaññi—"not another," "self."

118 Nârâyana } —the first man of great strength. [*Sk.* nara
Narâyana } or nâra + ayana.]

144 Abhidhâvati—"runs towards."

176 Vasî—"capable," "versed," "accomplished." [*Sk.* vaśin.]
Anukampâ—abl. of anukampa (*m.* or *n.*), "pity."

178 Jhâta—"known," "reputed," "thought of." [*Sk.* dhyâta.]

180 Ruta—P.P.P. of ruvati, from √ru, "to noise."

195 Salala } —*Pinus Longifolia.* [*Sk.* śarala.]
Salaḷa }
Ketaka (*m.*)—*Pandanus odoratissimus.*

196 Makula (*m.* or *n.*)—*Mimusops Elengi.*

201 Kûjati } —"warbles," "hums." √kuj and √kuc.
Kuñcati }

203 Seḷeti—"whistles."

207 Vijambhita (*n.*)—"sport," "gambol." [*Sk.* vijṛimbhita.]
Gîtî (*f.*)—"song."

208 Dhûpî (*f.*)—"perfume," "incense." √dhup.
Samphulla (as in *Sk.*)—"samphullito."

210 Sâmuddika—"marine."

211 Masâragallam (= masârakallaṁ)—"cat's-eye."

213 Khoma—"cloth from the Khoma country."

215 Kapiṭṭha = kaviṭṭha.
Coca—"palm fruit."

216 Ojaṁ (*n.*)—"essence."

221 Paroparaṁ (Vedic adv.) = paramparâ.

225 Orohanaka (*m.*) — "descent."

239 Lañchanaka = lañcanaka.

(C.) PROPER NAMES.

Anupîya—the mango grove in which Siddhattha sojourned on his way to Râjagaha.

Anomâ—the modern Rapti.

Âḷâra—Siddhattha's instructor after his renunciation.

Anitthigandha—an uxorious prince of Benares. *Vide* Notes, *v.* 89.

Udaka—Siddhattha's instructor after his renunciation.

Kanthaka—Siddhattha's horse.

Kusa—a king of Jambudîpa. *Vide* Notes, *v.* 88.

Channa—Siddhattha's servant.

Tusîta / Tussita—the fourth Devaloka.

Narâyana / Nârâyana—the first man of immense strength.

Pabhavati—daughter of King Madda, with whom Kusa fell in love. *Vide* Notes.

Ramma—the name of a city.

Ramma—Siddhattha's palace.

Lumbini—the grove in which Siddhattha was born, between Kapilavatthu and Devadaha.

Saṅkassa—a town of the Gangetic Doab; the place where Buddha descended after preaching to his mother in the Tâvatiṁsa heaven.

Sivinda—ruler of the Sivi people, *i.e.*, Vessantara.

Subbha—Siddhattha's palace.

Sumedha—the Bodhisat in the time of Dîpaṅkara.

Suramma—Siddhattha's palace.

Suyâma—the archangel who followed Siddhattha after his birth, holding the fan as a royal emblem.

Haritaco—a confidential adviser of the king of Benares. *Vide* Notes, *v.* 90.

(D.) RHETORICAL TERMS.

Abyâpeta = avyâpeta—"non-isolated," "undetached," "conjunct," used for rhyming words that come together.

Abyâpetâdiyamaka—"a rhyming word at the beginning of a quarter-verse." Abyâpetâdiyantayamaka—"conjunct rhymes at the beginning and end of a quarter-verse."

Akkharuttarika—"a letter passing beyond," *i.e.*, "alliterative."

Ekaṭhânikayamaka—"rhyme on one element," as, for example, on the gutturals in stanza 101. Rhymes may also be *dviṭhânika*, *tiṭhânika*, &c.

Paṭiloma—"palindromic." Paṭilomakaṁ—"palindrome."

Paheḷi—"enigmatic." Paheḷikâ (*f.*)—"enigma," "riddle."

Byâpeta = vyâpeta—"disjunct," "isolated." *Vide* "Abyapeta."

Byâsa = vyâsa—"distributed," diffused," applied to rhymes in no particular part of the *pâdas* of a stanza.

Yamaka—"rhyme," "synonymous sound." Mahâyamaka—"a stanza in which all the quarter-verses are the same." The following stanzas on "Yamaka" are from "Subodhâlaṅkâra:"—

> Yaṁ kiliṭṭhaṁ padaṁ mandâbhidheyyaṁ yamakâdikaṁ
> kiliṭṭhapadadose va tampi antokarîyati.
> Pattasaddaracitaṁ siliṭṭhapadasandhikaṁ
> pasâdaguṇasaṁyuttaṁ yamakaṁ matamedisaṁ.
> Abyâpetaṁ byâpetañca caññâvuttânekavaṇṇajaṁ
> yamakaṁ tañca pâdânamâdimajjhantagocaraṁ.
> Sujanâsujanâ sabbe guṇeṇâpi vivekino
> vivekaṁ na samâyanti aviveki janantike.
> Kusalâkusalâ sabbo pabalâpabalâtha vâ
> no yâtâ tâvâbosiṭṭhaṁ sukhadukkhappadâ siyuṁ.
> Sâdarasâdaraṁ hantu vihitâ vihitâ mayâ
> vandânavandanâmânabhâjaneratanatthaye.

Kamalaṁ kamalaṁkatthuṁ vanado vanadombaraṁ
sugato sugato lokaṁ sahitaṁ sahitaṁ karaṁ.
Abyâpetâdiyamakasseso leso nidassito
ñeyyânimayeva disâyaññâni yamakâni pi.
Accantabahavo tesaṁ bhedâ sambhedayoniyo
tattha pi keci sukarâ keci accantadukkarâ.
Yamakaṁ taṁ paheḷi ca nekantamadhurâni.

JINÂLAṄKÂRA

TRANSLATION

JINÂLAṄKÂRA

TRANSLATION.

1. The Buddha, most excellent in the three worlds, having abandoned wealth, children, wife, and bodily existence for mankind, having fulfilled the thirty *Pâramîs* and attained the unparalleled constituents of Transcendental Knowledge, attaining pure intelligence, which bestows all virtues—he, having put an end to suffering, has rescued virtuous people from misery.

2. Having paid honour to him, the Conqueror, abounding in accumulations of good, and the sole friend of the whole world, to whom most exalted in the world of creatures no one is equal in the potency of good, who is worthy of admiration, of extensive greatness, free from impurities and possessed of the essentials of Buddhaship, listen to me declaring the means, the appropriate means, tending to the Fruition leading to the state of Sugata.

3. He who is born in the ninth *Khaṇa* is full of knowledge, pure in his senses by the observance of the precepts, having looked upon transmigration with fear, and Nirvâṇa, the destroyer of existence, without fear—he, well worshipping the sage, because he points out the road tending to Bliss, should secure that bliss by means of the respective *bhâvanas*, *Buddhânussati*, &c.

4. Who is Buddha? What that Buddha virtue which is inconceivable and the like? What good has he not done

for the general weal? What has that Buddha declared and done which is not in accordance with truth and not held in common with others?

5. He is distinguished as Buddha as displaying the pure elements of being; and he, indeed, is distinguished as "possessed of good characteristics," who is pure in the display of the elements of existence.

6. Day by day, relying on his own supernatural power, he performed the Five Duties (incumbent on Buddhas), bringing faith to people; and, knowing fully the suitable conduct for them, preached the abandonment of the (seven) attachments.

7. He whose virtues are infinite and in the ascendency, he, being called the unparalleled sun in the threefold Buddha domain, knows this world and the future world, what is possessed of thought and what is devoid of thought, his own existence and that of others, as well as time past, future, and present.

8–10. Not one, nay, not all together in the endless world-systems are equal to him: in the different cardinal points, the east, &c., the worlds are innumerable owing to their existing in thousands, yet Devas, men, and Brahmas in them coming together and deliberating are not able to declare the road to Nirvâṇa, not knowing, by their own power, the rising up of corresponding Cause and Effect, of Name and Form antecedent in time without a beginning —not knowing their coming up and having entered into the various contrary conceptions, not knowing, too, the rise of action and consequence, whether single or multiple, produced or natural, being concealed by the density of intelligence and continuity, they are unable to declare the Way to Bliss.

11. He, the unparalleled light-giver and Bestower of Tranquillity, considering all that can be known, has the capability in the midst of them (Devas, men, and Brahmas) to show the Way to Bliss by publishing words, excellent and quieting.

12. The chief of Sages, of the Gotama family and the son of the Sakya race, being the Lamp of the whole world, has in virtue of his compassion caused endless people to escape from the bonds of existence, unregardful of anything in return.

13. Declare his inestimable goodness in this world! There is none equal to or surpassing him! How declare that goodness as given to him by a Buddha similar to himself, produced by himself, or whether obtained without a cause?

14. He has obtained this result of Buddhahood through the unparalleled acts of charity, &c., even self-performed—not obtained without a cause or from a previous Buddha, or by the authorisation of the large body of Brahmas and others.

15. In a past cycle, at the beginning of four *asaṅkkheyyas* and one hundred thousand *kappas*, when he was the hermit Sumedha, he went through the sky by supernatural power.

16, 17. When Dîpaṅkara, the Conqueror, went to the town of Ramma with his followers, being honoured by gods and men and shining (with glory) like the sun in the sky with a thousand rays, then, while those who were strenuously exerting themselves in making a path for him, he, Sumedha, on hearing the cry "Buddha," being pleased and delighted, said, "To-day, by giving up my body to him, I, like him, shall be a Buddha in the future."

18. On that track, having made his body into a bridge on the swampy mud, he, lying down, said, "If transcendental knowledge will be to me in the future, let this Buddha go over my head."

19. The Conqueror, Dîpankara, went towards his head, knowing his intention would be realised in the future, and made an unqualified prediction, saying, "He indeed will become Buddha in the future."

20. On hearing this, he, as if having attained the state of one who received the sprinkling (of purification), and imagining supernatural knowledge as obtained by him, rose and acquired a complete grasp of the ten *Pâramîs* after the sage (Dîpankara) as well as Devas and men had honoured him and gone away.

21. Having obtained firm mastery in all the thirty *Pâramîs*, and though he had the power to attain Nirvâṇa by passing beyond existence, through Dîpankara possessed of the three *sikkhâs*, he, through pity for creatures, transmigrated.

22. He having paid full honour to the various peerless Buddhas who have made their appearance, it having been predicted by them with certainty that he would be a Buddha, adored with his head the peerless words of those Buddhas, and, bearing up every suffering, he fulfilled the *Pâramîs* which bestow all good qualities.

23. He who, oppressed by suffering, saw people too oppressed by suffering, always manifested compassion for mankind, knew verily such and such to be the means of their emancipation, and laid their sin upon himself.

24. By sinking in the seas of the various excellent *Pâramîs*, charity, &c., he, seeking the benefit of creatures, did not consider even the suffering entailed upon him by wicked men as anything considerable.

25. Severing his own head and giving it, cooking his own flesh and giving it, he, during the time of his aspirations for Buddhaship, having abandoned his body—how could he offend the wicked by such sacrifice?

26. Thus seeking the benefit of creatures, he underwent endless suffering during a hundred births; and, in the time of Dîpankara, devoted himself to wisdom, mental concentration, and the precepts, until he accomplished his aim at the foot of his own Bodhi tree.

27. When Sumedha (in the time of Dîpankara) made aspirations towards Buddhahood, and when he, as Sivinda, gave up Madî, there was not, within the births of these two periods, even a single benefit which he did not attain.

28. His births during that time being as countless as the innumerable drops of water in the great ocean—how can be expressed the endless extent of his accomplished *Pâramîs*, or where can there be found a similarity to him?

29. He who has sown the seed of a sweet mango on the roadside with the object of providing shade and fruit, even in the very moment of sowing it, in virtue of the shade and the fruit (he intends to provide), there is acquired by him whatever merit had not been obtained before.

30. So, when he (Sumedha) planted himself for the benefit of mankind on the road of transmigration, over him there sprang up merit, and whoever wished divested him of his wealth, his limbs, and life.

31. He gave more blood than there is water in the ocean; he gave as offering his own flesh exceeding the earth in quantity, his head with its crested hair surpassing Mount Meru in size, and his eyes exceeding in number the stars in the sky.

32, 33. Crossing verily by his power over the deep oceans of the water of charity, &c., and bringing the *Pâramîs* to a consummation by the bestowal of Madî; living among the multitude in the Tusita heaven and attaining to the maturity of knowledge, he, at the request of the Devas, entered his mother's womb.

34. With thought and consciousness he entered his mother's womb; at the time of his entering it, the ten thousand worlds quaked.

35. Then at the time when he was in the womb there were visible the thirty-two characteristics of a great man: the mother, enraptured, sees her son in the womb.

36. She, on coming to her full time, after ten months, went to the excellent Lumbini grove in bloom, stood holding the excellent branch of a tree, and easily gave birth to that excellent son.

37. Then Devas and Nâgas, Asuras and Yakkhas, of the ten thousand worlds, from all sides came in raptures of delight to the blessed world-system.

38. The Devas held up in the sky branches of various kinds, and an umbrella, a thousand in circumference; gold-handled whisps flap; they beat drums, and conches sound.

39. Unbesmeared with any filth, he stood spreading out his feet and appeared like a preacher descending from a pulpit, or the excellent sun coming out from a cloud.

40. Sinless hosts of Brahmas approached him and received him in a net of gold, the Devas in the hide of the antelope, and men in the finest cloth.

41. Leaving their hands, he stood on the excellent spot of ground: he looked fully at all the points of the compass, and Devas as well as Brahmas said, "Equal to thee or superior there is no one anywhere!"

42. Making an advance of seven paces northward he sent forth a pleasant shout, causing those Devatas to hear him.

43. The mother then went to her home, taking her son; and on the seventh day she attained the state of Deva.

44. The Brahmas, having regaled themselves well with food, on seeing, on the fifth day, his excellent characteristics in order to give him a name, raised one finger and said, "He will be a Buddha devoid of sin:"

45. "On seeing an old man, a sick man, a dead man swathed in cloth, and a monk, he, abandoning the pleasures of sense, enters upon the ascetic life and will become a Buddha free from sin."

46, 47. In course of time increasing (in beauty, &c.) in the prospering family like the moon, and advancing in merit like the sun in the sky, Siddhattha—named so because he had accomplished every good—having obtained Yasodhara as his wife, was attended by forty thousand accomplished women.

48. During the three seasons of the year, in suitable dwellings—the Ramma, the Suramma, and the Subha palaces—he pleasurably enjoyed the wonderful and astonishing magnificence of royalty like the bliss of the celestial world.

Honour to him, inasmuch as to him possessed of greatness no darkness is!

49. On seeing the (four) signs for the destruction of pride, the uncomeliness of women for the destruction of enjoyment, evil deeds for the destruction of happiness, there was acquired by him the knowledge for the destruction of existence.

50. The great sage, on seeing his wife and son, did not give vent to the great torrent of his love, like one rising up and going away, making a terrible uproar, from a blazing house.

51. Going and removing his foot from the threshold of Mâra, the most excellent of men, on his way to Nirvâṇa, thought to himself, "It is fit for me to go by the raft of adorning goodness: the wish comes to me very much for the destruction of sin."

52. The great sage, going to the threshold of Mâra, reflected well about the breaking up of pollution, saying, "What benefit to me remaining in the mouth of death and old age? there is no profit remaining in the realm of desire—not in my own domain."

53. "Not by the various desires is there the consummation of freedom; there is no benefit to me by pride in its various forms; Mâra with his army, not easy to be checked, crushes me like one crushing sugar-cane with a pressing machine."

54. Seeing men burning (with *Kilesas*), roaming about (in transmigration), carried away (by the four floods), base, without protection, without refuge, without asylum, and not seeing happiness, he thought, "How can they be instructed by me (if) devoted to sensual inclinations?"

55. "I who have attached myself to wisdom, separated myself from ignorance, and am regardless of attachments, I am unable to take over mankind (across the ocean of transmigration) whether with or without essential good, or whether separated from wisdom or attached to ignorance."

56. "The unorthodox do not declare Nirvâṇa to be the road (to Bliss); these men are unanimous in calling heresy superior: the society of one who is in the darkness of

ignorance is bare: I shall destroy that society by the most excellent path of Saintship."

57. "By violent action men produce suffering that cannot be borne: they know not that insufferable evil has its origin in their violence of action."

58. "The *oghas, yogas, âsavas*, and *kilesas* which rise up destroy men: birth, decay, and death are certain; and misfortune of various kinds is perpetuated."

59. For a long time seeing the blazing of the fire of *kilesas* and knowing the inner thoughts of creatures, the self-instructed one thought—"I will attain to the perfection of knowledge; I will instruct creatures and afterwards I shall behold that renowned son of mine."

60. "The celestial wheel is like a razor worn as a fillet round the head, sovereignty like something to be disgusted with, the society (of women) like a society of drunkards, the relations coming to place me in bondage like enemies, this son born to me the Ambassador of Impurity:"

61. "Her existent glory abides blazing in her; this is like a great serpent's hole and a great poison; these brilliant young women are like a thorny fence in the pure path to Nirvâṇa."

62. "To whose glory no other glory can be compared, on looking at whom (Yasodhara) there is no end to satiety—Now Desire, I shall undertake the breaking of thy head; I shall go on the majestic lion-like path over the temporal cavity of the elephant intoxicated with lust:"

63. "O Sir, Desire, for a long time the discharger of arrows, bundle up your arrows; henceforth destroy what has been discharged; and by repelling you with a mind

that has attained to the absence of any footing (for existence) grieve not; but even if grieving, I shall go to Bliss without looking at thee, O Desire:"

64. "Delight and pleasure in sensuality be off! in seclusion (from the world) delight is befitting; thus reflecting, I, rending the mind attached to Desire, depart as a girl seeing a snake somewhere."

65. As long as the sun travels impeded by the Cakkavâḷa rock and the Cakkaratana goes along (unobstructed) in the world, till then how can he, going in the sky as lord and conqueror of the Four Islands bounded by the Cakkavâḷa, forsake all and, being free from attachment, remove his foothold from the world?

66. Forsaking the four great islands and the 2000 lesser islands, and in them the excellent Jambudîpa, supplied with fruits and occupied by the most exalted of beings, and the delightful town of Kapilavastu in the centre of the Earth, how did he, without desires, withdraw his foot?

67. Abandoning eighty thousand of his relatives of the Sakya family, who, since seven generations, had conquered crowds of enemies and who were in possession of elephants, horses, corn and wealth,—abandoning the chief of men, his father, superior to all the house of Gotama—how did he, free from attachments, remove his foothold?

68. Having abandoned his beautiful Suramma edifice, resplendent with gems, in summer most wonderful, being as splendid as a Deva's abode, having abandoned the flag and steamer and the white umbrella raised aloft, how did he, free from desires, remove his foothold?

69. Having forsaken the four tanks with the lotuses that flourished in the vicinity of his dwelling—(cranes sing on the red lotuses)—how did he, free from desires, upraise his foot?

70. He sees around the palace from his window the row of bees that buzz on the lotuses on the lake; seeing their lord's mouth, a veritable lotus, the lotuses recoil, as it were, through shame.

71. The bees went about on the various lotuses happy and with pleasant buzz; they even now besmeared his palace with honey, crying, "Why was this (dwelling) abandoned by our Lord?"

72. The bees, carrying the nectar thence to the palace with resounding sounds, manufacture most delectable honey; the women play on the lute in sounds surpassing the music of the bees; they then dance like the females in the Devaloka.

73. The virtuous (women), with brilliant metallic zones and plump inviting breasts and lips, afford pleasure like celestial fairies: these charmers, like medicine, bring happiness to men.

74. The charming women, delighting in pleasure, beat drums, &c., with hands highly reddened, in the vicinity of the palace: a thousand advance dancing with instruments in their hands and incite him, saying, "Though Sakka exist, what equal is there to one of the Sakya race?"

75. The charming well-dressed women, well decked and bearing garlands of flowers, with voices astonishingly harmonious, breasts like the Nimba, beautiful waists, and eyes large, dance to the resounding accompaniment of drums.

76. Women to whom in the world there were no equals, whose touch language has no power to describe—partaking of such sensual enjoyments and forsaking them, how did he, free from desire, upraise his foot?

77. She (Yasodhara) sings songs already learnt or extempore, giving pleasure to her master, sending out harp-like sounds from her girdle and anklet, with the feet on the ground or thrown up in the air: the women whirl about to movements of the bracelets, with hands uplifted or lowered: seeing this joy-making, yet without seeing it, he goes away—Alas! alas! what benefit in all these efforts?

78. By merit through an endless accumulation of time, he, on that day, forsaking his begotten son, his wife as well as his vehicles and residences acquired by him, departed as if he was Sugata (Tathâgata) who had attained Nirvâṇa.

79. Forsaking his living father and (step) mother, such relatives and such females (as have been referred to), as well as such habitations, he departed like Tathâgata gone to Nirvâṇa.

80. Clad in well-scented robes of Kâsi and China, of Khoma and Pattuna, and in the *dukûla*, he was as resplendent as Sakka! Forsaking all this, he departed like Tathâgata gone to Nirvâṇa.

81. The four jars of treasures that display the lustre of greatness rose up from the earth which holds creatures on its surface—the earth containing inanimate as well as animate beings, and on which dwell the eaters of ambrosia. Forsaking these, he departed like Tathâgata gone to Nirvâṇa.

82. He ate Sâli rice, good and sweet-smelling, along with the women, his charming fellow-dwellers, from a golden tray decorated with a hundred lines; but leaving this, he departed like Tathâgata gone to Nirvâṇa.

83. His body, naturally perfumed with grateful odours, was anointed with odorous perfumes, and fanned with fragrant air; forsaking this, he departed like Tathâgata gone to Nirvâṇa.

84. He had his body excellently marked with beautiful signs and decorated with god-like ornaments, and he was resplendent with princesses of the same race. Forsaking all this, he departed like Tathâgata gone to Nirvâṇa.

85. Various seats, sleeping-places, residences as brilliant as the stars and like the ocean, the Repository of Gems, and there the upraised flag adorned with gems,—these he abandoned,—these which he considered like drops of dew.

86. He has gone from the women resplendent with various gems; from his residences always musical with their voices, and from his sovereignties adorned with the *cakkaratana:* he, indeed, in consequence, is honoured by the most excellent of men.

87. He, indeed, has gone away like Tathâgata having abandoned Yasodhara with full lips and breasts, having limbs like the flags in the theatre of Anaṅga, resplendent with the splendour of celestial nymphs, and dutiful to her husband.

88. Prince Kusa having served Pabhâvati, who had no natural desire for enjoyments, carried the rice-pole: forsaking the beautiful and excellent Yasodhara, superior to her, he verily departed like Tathâgata.

89. Anitthigandha formerly, desiring the wives of others, went about in the town armed with a sword; though abandoning dignity, he did not abandon women, but now, forsaking this Yasodhara, he, the Tathâgata, departed.

90. Haritaca, through force of his passion on account of the nakedness of the queen, ignored his vow of chastity and followed his desires, but now forsaking such enjoyment he, the Bodhisat, has assuredly departed as the Tathâgata.

91. Practising separation from the world during countless cycles, he went away, abandoning royal magnificence and a most excellent woman: he described that past sacrifice as a small stake, looking upon it as a tailor looks upon a hole in a garment.

92. Bearing this in mind, the God of Love now praised Yasodhara, who was like the flag (in his theatre); and he, the kinsfolk of remissness, said, "He who is intoxicated with passion is conquered by me:" he knew not of the occasion for the discharge of the thunderbolt of knowledge.

93. Seeing existence as the origin of the fire of suffering and destroying lust that gives rise to it, he abandoned Yasodhara with plump lips and breast, and attained Nirvâṇa which gives potency to Buddhas.

94. Having had a hold on the minds of endless creatures, during endless ages, the (hitherto) victorious God of Love was indeed overcome by him singly: he who went away thus (to become a monk) will not return.

95. Seeing the occasion for the discharge of the thunderbolt of knowledge, he, the God of Love, having thus undergone defeat, will not return again.

96. His going away (after the conquest of Anaṅga) was wonderful; wonderful indeed the bringing about of the cessation of combustion; wonderful, too, when Mâra spoke of the Buddha's attainment of tranquillity; wonderful, indeed, when he did not set his mind on the laughter, &c., of the daughters of Mâra.

97. The renouncer of his life together with desires, attained to the end of his intention by means of restraint; the giver of his life together with desires, attained Nirvâṇa by various means; he, not allowing himself *Kilesas* with

Kâma attained, by diverse means, to perfect knowledge; he who attained to perfect knowledge gave mankind their desires.

98. The Jina, without enmity at the harsh speech in the struggle with Mâra, caused the terror-stricken criers (suffering in hell, &c.), like one trembling (as the sun) in regard to an enemy (Râhu), by means of utterances well spoken and supplications reverential, to know utterances free from enmity.

99. The time of thy coming into the world was specially distinguished: the time of thy going out from the world was specially distinguished as well.

100. The dignity with which the King of Kings is endowed has been treated of by me: I, full of religious fervour, until I attain undecay, will resort to him, whom without decay, I have long served.

101. O Possessor of senses for the obtaining of desires, of a bodily organisation for the dispersion of doubt, not a believer in the river of doubt, but the destroyer of doubts in those who hold them—Alas! alas! where can there be doubt in me?

102. He is without future conception, without the incidents of conception (name and form), without delusion (ignorance), and does not produce delusion in others: he has preached emancipation obtainable by entrance into the Chief Path (*i.e.*, by the gateway of Saintship): he has not preached the augmentation of delusion.

103. Seeing the existence of merit and demerit, he went away from merit and demerit; merit and demerit being attachments, he went away from merit and demerit.

104. Seeing the existence of merit and demerit, he relinquished merit and demerit; from unattachment to merit and demerit, he departed from merit and demerit.

105. To our living one surely are no imperfections, no corruptions; no faults to our living one that have not been removed; no mouth is equal to the mouth of our Lord.

106. The Lord of the Lake of the Essences of Sweet Juices, who is the remembrancer of worldlings and celestials in religious essentials, is the filler of the lake-like heads of worldlings and celestials with the best of the essences among the essences of Sweet Juices.

107. Sakka, pleasing to the gods, was not pleased with the God of Gods (Buddha), owing to his own deficiency of knowledge; Buddha by his knowledge understood the thoughts of Sakka; Sakka, by his own knowledge, knew his own weakness.

108. Seated on the Deva throne, he, the Deva of Devas, pointed out to the seated gods and men the food of knowledge in his religion.

109. Buddha, the name that proceeds from the lips, is the sun that destroys the darkness of ignorance; let him who has accomplished his aim by the attainment of Saintship, protect me like himself.

110. The great sage is indeed devoted to his own as well as the good of others; indeed by the potency of the ten *Pâramîs*, and verily by the destruction of Mâra's army, he assuredly attained to the purest knowledge.

111. Having descended from the palace divested of evil, he, the illustrious being, went on his horse (Kanthaka), well trapped, along with Channa to the bank of the Anoma, and attained to the illustrious state of a monk.

112. In the Anûpiya mango grove he obtained the most unequalled joy and happiness of an ascetic life, free from objects of desire; Râjagaha, with its sovereignty, he looked upon as devoid of splendour, through the natural splendour of his personality.

113. Then being displeased with the Jhâna of Âḷâra and Udaka, the hermits, he proceeded to Uruveḷa for his great exertion (in the path of Buddhahood), and practised the highest order of penance.

114. "From attachment to desires I cannot practise the highest penance; omniscience is accomplished by the mediocre path of Saintship." Knowing this, he went to the excellent Tree of Knowledge to produce the state of *Samâdhi* which was productive of former virtues.

115. Having obtained the white umbrella in the three Buddha Fields, he might be the Lord of the universe; so going forth he sat for his fight with Mâra unmovable on the unconquerable seat under the Tree of Knowledge.

116. Parting with his sovereignty over men, his father, Suddhodhana, then paid honour to him with the white umbrella, adoring him with his head.

117. The Mahâbrahmâ, Sahaṁpati, gave up his sovereignty in his dominion with Devas and Brahmas together, and paid honour with the white umbrella.

118. Gotama himself, as powerful as Nârâyana, attained the potentiality of Highest Knowledge, and came to the throne at the Tree of Knowledge to conquer the whole world.

119. Then King Vasavatti, Lord of the Six Kâma Worlds, accompanied by his army, approached the throne at the Tree of Knowledge.

120. "Come," said he, "seize, bind, cast off this low-born; he thinks not 'I am a worm born in a human fœtus.'"

121. He caused a ninefold blazing shower to fall, created a blinding smoke, incalculable in volume, and threw many thunderbolts.

122. Throwing also his circular weapon he could effect nothing; seeing no other weapon that could be brought to use, he spoke thus:

123. "Siddhattha! wherefore art thou in my own rightful seat? get up from it; if not, I shall split thy heart."

124. As a father seeing his young son playing at his feet, he looked at Mâra displaying love and exercising compassion.

125. Then the Sage shouted out in sounds fearless but pleasant (lion-like)—"This base one knows not of himself that he is my slave!"

126. "By whatever Kamma he was born in the excellent celestial city, not knowing about his own coming into it, he imagines himself *chief of the world!*"

127. "Indeed the good done by men in the innumerable world-systems is not worth a sixteenth part of even one of the *Pâramîs* (practised by me)."

128. "While I was the animal hare, on seeing a mendicant coming, I fell into the fire, cooking my flesh to offer it."

129. "Thus was performed by me actions of penance during endless ages; who other (than Mâra), indeed, possessed of intelligence, and not insane, could have acted thus (in coming into conflict with me)?"

130. "And so, one, not knowing in reality that this body is brought into being (produced) by endless good actions, imagines me a man, saying, 'Thou art a man!'"

131. "I am neither a man nor a demon, not a Brahmâ nor a Devatâ; I have come here (to the Bodhi tree) to point out death and decay to the world."

132. "I, the conqueror of endless things, uncontaminated by the world—the Buddha at the foot of the Tree of Knowledge—cause many people to cross over (to Nirvâṇa)."

133. Seeing warring Mâra with standards all around, he said, "I go forth to the battle; let him not expel me from my place."

134. "Thy army, which the world of men together with the gods could not overcome, that, thine army, I shall go through by means of Wisdom just as an unbaked bowl is broken through with a stone."

135. "If wishing it, I can go about in the cavity of a sessamum seed; wishing it, I covered the universe with my body."

136. "I have the energy and strength to take them in an instant and crush them to powder, but the taking of life is not right."

137. "Of what use armed force towards this worm? converse with such an evil one is also, verily, not befitting."

138. "The throne is a thing for myself; what benefit by a witness? the earth which shook owing to the giving away of Madî is a witness."

139. Having spoken so, he inclined his right hand towards the ground: then the earth shook and a great noise uprose.

140. Along with the terrestrial noise there burst in the sky a thunderbolt, making a roaring noise; it fell in mid-air; Mâra, along with his attendants, was terror-stricken.

141. The army was scattered like dust thrown up by a strong wind: a great sound was produced—"This is the victory of Siddhattha!"

142. The moon goes from the east like a silver wheel in the sky; the sun with a thousand rays descends in the west.

143. Seated cross-legged on the unconquerable throne, under the Tree of Knowledge as an umbrella, in the centre of the earth, the Sage grasped the Law.

144. Just then Sakka runs blowing his conch; Brahmâ holds an umbrella of three leagues over the Sage's head.

145. A Deva of the Tusita heaven held a ruby-like palm fan, Suyâma the tail-whisp, and the rest of the Devas held various auspicious gifts.

146. Thus Sakka, Brahmâ, and the Devas in the ten thousand world-systems filled up the world (in which Buddha was), blowing conches, &c.

147. Some celestials stand holding auspicious gifts, some holding flags and garlands, some, likewise, holding full water-jars, &c.

148. The celestials of the ten thousand world-systems dance, sing, whistle, and play upon musical instruments, and through ecstasy are filled with joy.

149. Said they, "We shall obtain the luscious nectar of the Law, the luscious ambrosia of his eyes, and we shall witness wonders."

150. He, pointing out the way to Nirvâṇa, liberated mankind from the stakes of sorrow and desperation, from the thorny path of old age and death, and from the trap of desire.

151. Thus the most excellent of men, honoured by the delighted gods, was not thinking of any honour (paid to him), thinking of the excellent Law.

152–155. Siddhattha, having accomplished his desires and not being overcome, remembered his previous birth in the first watch, seated on the unconquerable throne, under the jewel-like umbrella of the Tree of Knowledge on the Bodhi throne, in the Cakkavâḷa as a palace resonant with joyous singing and the beating of celestial festival drums, honoured with garlands and perfumes under the canopy of the sky decked with stars and brilliant with various ornaments, and beautiful from the Cakkavâḷa rocks serving as screens and walls.

156. Thereby the springing up in this world of Name and Form was well perceived by him; the heresy recognising body as his own was in consequence completely abandoned by him.

157. Then in the second watch, he brought to mind the enterings of creatures into new existences in accordance with the law of *Karma;* consequently the origin of existence through *Karma* and *Kilesa* became perfectly manifest to him.

158. The knowledge called *Kaṅkhâvitaraṇî* (the Dispeller of Doubt) was attained; by that the sixteen-fold doubts that exist disappeared completely.

159. After that, he the Sage, in the third watch, caused his knowledge to settle on the twelve-fold Chain of Causation.

160. Touching upon Ignorance, &c., in consecutive order, and on old age, &c., in opposite order, he arrived at true insight.

161, 162. During innumerable births, calculated by hundreds of Koṭis, by repeatedly destroying the desire of acquisition by complete liberality, he put a stop to anger and enmity by observance of the precepts, by forbearance, and by love, by means of wisdom severing delusion and, likewise, false belief.

163–165. By serving those worthy of respect and the like dispelling doubt, by respect to elders in his family, getting rid of pride and presumption, repeatedly destroying desire by the renunciation of the world, falsehood by truth, and indolence by energy,—thus by charity, &c., getting rid of every component of sin (*Kilesa*), how should not such great well-increasing wisdom grow into the tranquillity of Nirvâṇa?

166. In the performance of difficult duties in the past, such as charity and the like, he desired not the grandeurs of existence; he aspired to excellent Buddhahood.

167. From his aspirations (in the time of Dîpaṅkara), his longings as well as the meritorious acts performed by him, taken together now, undoubtedly give him complete knowledge.

168. Then touching upon all the elements of being, he, in the light of impermanence, suffering and unreality taken consecutively, attained Nirvâṇa.

169. Burning up his taints to the very smallest particle with their accompanying impressions, he, by the attainment of Saintship, became the pure Buddha at the foot of the Tree of Knowledge.

170. Having obtained the excellent white umbrella of Saintship, he, in the precipitancy of his joy, gave expression to the intensity of his feelings; having rent asunder the *Máras* and having conquered the whole body of his enemies, he became the unrivalled Sun in the three Buddha Fields.

171. He was indeed excellent of all, being King of Kings; holding three umbrellas, he was the excellent King of Law; he had the power with his voice to instruct not only one world-system, but a thousand world-systems.

172, 173. What born creature is without sense in the worlds in which Buddha is the light (of knowledge)? Who wise and full of faith would not adore him the pure Buddha crossed over from the flood, who is deserving to be served, who has forsaken taints, who is air and life, who has renounced the world, seized the truth, who is attractive and untainted, who goes on the right path and avoids the wrong road, who goes on the road to righteousness, not on that of evil, deserving to be adored, immeasurable, not ignorant, but wise?

174. "Verily attaining purity beyond the purity of others, the destruction of all taint and the highest knowledge is an excellent attainment indeed;" thinking so continually about perfect knowledge for seven days, he, even during that time, enjoyed various happiness—the fruit of Saintship—and on being asked by Brahmá he set forth the supreme truths of religion in the Isipatana wood.

175. What man, indeed, possessed of sense would not adore his preaching, beneficial and real, full of love and truth, capable of instructing up to one's desires, expressed in the tones of the cuckoo and in the voice of a Brahmá?

176. Bhagavâ became proficient in three wonders—supernatural power, religious instruction, and admonition. Having attained to these astonishing wonders, he, through compassion, pointed out the Law to this world.

177. Verily, thus having attained Buddhahood, he, in various ways, pointed out the Law to men and gods; he gave surpassing enlightenment to sentient beings, and therefore is he reputed as the Lord of the Three Existences.

178. The Devas and Brahmas praised Buddha, having, verily, attained the light of Law, seen, acquired, and recognised the Truth, and having crossed over from attachment, hatred, and ignorance.

179. He is the most excellent King of Sages, the most excellent King of men, the most excellent Deva among Devas, the purest Brahmâ, the remover of his own evil and the remover of the evil of others, the augmenter of his own advantage and the augmenter of the advantages of others.

180. The qualities, *Araha*, &c., spoken of by Devas, Brahmas, and men, being extensive and pure, are ninefold, accepted on the earth and in the sky, and are spread abroad in the whole of the Deva worlds and in the three existences.

181. The Buddha characteristics are indeed the incomprehensibility, &c., of the Honoured One, surpassing in purity the purity of others; they fall concisely into nine heads; I shall now set forth the qualities of *Araha*, &c.

182. He who was born here, worthy to be honoured, free from desire, perfectly wise and omniscient, replete with good practices and learning, who has crossed the Flood, has come well, goes under the name of Sugata.

183. He knew this world and the others; he was the excellent horseman for the subjugation of men; he carried out the excellent duties of Teacher in relation to gods and men; he was wise (in the knowledge of the Four Truths), full of glory and pure.

184. There is nothing here not visible to him, nothing, moreover, not known or not to be known; he knows everything that can be known; therefore is the Tathâgata omniscient.

185. Thus, here (in the world) should be contemplated that excellent Buddha knowledge of distinguished essential elements, infinite and worthy of reverence, unlimited by time, and ever the means of the production of merit in all the ten thousand world-systems.

186. By him who is wise listening to the scriptures and their exposition, requiring the exercise of reflection, there is comprehended that essential and pure discourse; indeed, realising well the good consequences by results, the cause is known by him; and, in consequence, by great efforts, he believes also in the omniscience produced in the Buddha.

187. And he who believing in his omniscience recites his attributes—*worthiness to be honoured*, &c.—according as stated, and reflects on them, he soon forsakes evil and attains to the tranquillity of Nirvâṇa.

188. They (who do this) are to be believed, to be thought about, worshipped and honoured; they, by aspiring to this (position), are born in the world in which Buddha is the world's light.

189. Therefore, I worship him, the honoured of honoured ones in the past, by means of existing attractive things in the store-room of his birth, in the auspicious world-system appertaining to a Buddha.

190. I now pay honour to scentless and unscentless flowers produced on water or on land, growing in this world-system,

191. In the various ponds and tanks in the gardens of men in it, in the Himalayan wood or in its seven great lakes;

192. To the flowers that flourish in the great island as well as in the two thousand smaller islands, on the seven circular rocks and on the excellent Mount Meru—

193. The kumuda, uppala, and other lotuses in the abodes of the Dragons, the trumpet-flower, &c., in the dwelling of the Titans,

194. The Koviḷâra, &c., too, in the dwelling of the Gods, and various such-like flowers growing on the earth—

195. The campaka, salala, nâga, punnâga, ketaka, vassika, mallika, sâla, koviḷâra, and pâṭali,

196. Indivâra, asoka, kaṇikâra, makula, paduma, puṇḍarika, and sweet-scented kumuda and uppala:

197. These, as well as others, trees as well as creepers, those that grow sweet-smelling, soft to the touch, of various colours and beautiful,

198. Variegated, of different shades of dark, yellow, red, black, white, brown, beautiful plants of various colours.

199. The Himalaya, the repository of gems, is attractive with flowing rivers, streaks of forests, and with lakes under the mountain.

200. The forest is bespread with pollen from the pericarp of the petals; bees, owing to the perfume of flowers around, hum loudly.

201. Birds, too, are there; these twice-born creatures are sweet-voiced and beautiful; the warblers warble on the trees which blossom in season.

202. The mountains resound with the descent of immortals; and there are heard instruments like the five kinds of celestial musical instruments.

203. There the Kinnaras, beautifully decorated like the fairies among the gods, dance, sing, whistle, and play (on musical instruments).

204. The golden-coloured mountains there blaze like flames of fire; there indeed work is performed by the Kinnara by means of the mountain-lamp.

205. On account of the descent of the gods, rubies, opals, &c., remain sparkling and appear like nets of pearls:

206. The brown sandal-wood, taggara, camphor, green sandal-wood, are there; the place is replete with the sound of birds, the cry of peacocks,

207. With the hum of bees, the roar of elephants, the sporting of beasts of prey, the singing of Kinnaras,

208. With the radiance of the mountains, the splendour of the rubies, with variegated ethereal canopies, and with the perfume of flowers of the trees. Thus replete with all elements, what can the Nandana wood be (in comparison)?

209. There being thus the various well-blooming forests, and in them the beautiful flowering trees as well as agreeable sounds and pleasant odours, (with these) I worship him, honoured before by those deserving to be honoured.

210. In the dragon world, in that of men, Devas, and Brahmas, whatever wealth there might be in the ocean, the earth or the sky—

211. Silver, gold, pearl, opal, emerald, the speckled ruby, crystal, red ruby, and the coral—

212. This wealth I offer to him, the Buddha, who fulfilled the Ten Perfections during countless cycles, and taught the Four Truths to beings.

213. Khoma and silk, cotton and sâṇa, hempen and woollen stuffs, the celestial dukûla garments—these various kinds—

214. By the endless bestowal of which in charity the discipline of shame and modesty was perfected in the Buddha—with these garments I worship him.

215. The most exquisite juice of various fruits of trees growing in the forest—mangoes, wood-apples, jacks, and endless kinds of palm fruits and plantains.

216. The sweet-smelling juice as well as essence in them having been offered by me, I adore him always with my head with a serene mind.

217. I pay honour to his first inconceivable aspiration (to Buddhahood) by means of all the existing objects in the world-system.

218. I pay honour to the excellent spot of the consummation of the Ten Perfections; then to his last birthplace in the delightful Sâla wood.

219. I adore the severe practices in his religious efforts during six years, the unconquerable throne, his perfect knowledge, and the attributes of Buddha.

220. I adore the fourteen *Buddhañâṇas*, the eighteen *Âveṇikas*, the ten *Balañâṇas*, the four excellent *Vesârajjas*.

221. The *Âsaya* and *Anusaya Ñâṇas*, the knowledge of the successive orders of sentient beings, the *Yamakapâṭihîras* and the *Sabbaññutaññâṇa*,

222. The *Mahâkaruṇâpattiñâṇa* and the *Anâvaraṇañâṇa* —I bow down to these six uncommon powers and adore them.

223. I then pay honour to the Law grasped in seven weeks, as well as to the place where he was asked by Brahma to point out the excellent Law.

224. I pay honour to the establishment of the rule of religion in the deer-park of the Isipatana wood; moreover, I adore his residence in the monastery of the Bamboo grove.

225. I then pay honour to the beautiful Jetavan, resided in for a long time by the great Sage, and to the *Yamakapâṭihariya*, not found in common with others.

226. I honour the preaching of the Abhidhamma at the foot of the Coral tree as well as his descent from the Deva world at the town-gate of Saṅkassa.

227. Moreover, I bow down and adore the *Mahâsamaya* discourse on the Himalayan mountain as well as at those places mentioned by me.

228. In the way above mentioned, I pay honour to the Scriptures composed of eighty-four thousand scriptural sections.

229. I adore his renunciation of the elements of existence to Mâra between the two Sâla trees in Kusinârâ belonging to the Malla princes.

230. The taintless one, from the time of his aspiration (to Buddhahood), having completed all that had to be done, attained Nirvâṇa.

231. The great long-standing compassion of him who had thus performed what had to be done and had attained Nirvâṇa did not die out.

232, 233. The great Sage enjoined—"After my death, let this Dhamma and Vinaya, well shown to you by me, as well as my bodily relics, be your teacher; let also the unconquerable throne and the excellent Tree of Knowledge be your teacher."

234. Having set the Tree of Knowledge and my relics in my place, I permit you their worship for the purpose of your attainment of the road to Nirvâṇa."

235. Therefore I bow down and worship, considering—"He who is Sambuddha, having acquired it, teaches his excellent Law according to the truth."

236. So I bow down and adore without exception every relic of the Buddha in the extensive Cakkavâḷa, even to the amount of a mustard seed.

237. I bow down to and adore all the Bodhi trees perpetuated in succession from this (first) Bodhi tree.

238. Whatever articles, bowls, robes, &c., the Revered One used—all these used relics I bow down to and adore.

239. Wherever he lay down, wherever he was seated in the arcade, or wherever he left his footprint—I bow down and adore.

240. Whatever images are made in order to know Buddha's nature for those who do not know him—I bow down to them all and adore them.

241. Thus I honour the excellent Buddha, the Law, and the Priesthood by means of all things in the world-systems.

242. May I be deserving of love in every existence, owing to mortifications, ceremonial observances, and all meritorious acts performed by me in this existence as well as in my previous existence.

243. May faith, modesty, fear of sinning and great knowledge, energy, thoughtfulness, concentration of mind and surpassing wisdom, like Indra's thunderbolt possessed of the virtue of penetration, be consummated in me until my attainment of Buddhahood.

244. Having got rid of desire, hatred and illusion, heresy, pride, and doubt, and being free from niggardliness, jealousy, and impurity, may I be stable and devoid of conceit.

245. May I not be oppressed by any one, but be wealthy and not humiliated through garments given in gifts to me; may the wealth and body obtained by me be, forsooth, for the benefit of others.

246. May I support my parents according to the Law and, being respectful to elders and of great service (to others), may I bring about the advancement of myself as well as that of relatives, friends, and enemies.

247. Having approached the Protector Meteyya, I shall pay honour to his person, and acquiring the excellent *Veyyâkaraṇa*, I shall be Buddha in future times.

248. Not being polluted by the world, delighting in charity, established in the precepts and virtues, undergoing renunciation of the world, and obtaining excellent knowledge, may I be replete with strength and power.

249. May I exercise forbearance in the cutting off of my head and flesh, hands and feet; being established in

truth, may I be devoted to love and equanimity in order to be steadfast.

250. Having made the five great sacrifices and, not missing the road to omniscience, having severed moral depravities, and being victorious over the five Mâras, shall I be Buddha in future times.

THE END.

www.ingramcontent.com/pod-product-compliance
Lightning Source LLC
Chambersburg PA
CBHW032146010726
47493CB00008BA/2603